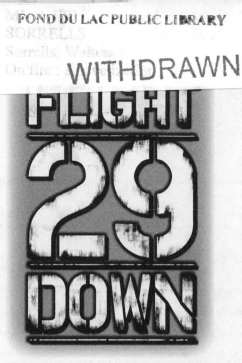

FLIGHT 29 DOWN

On Fire

Stan Rogow Productions · Grosset & Dunlap

GROSSET & DUNLAP
Published by the Penguin Group
Penguin Group (USA) Inc., 375 Hudson Street, New York, New York 10014, U.S.A.
Penguin Group (Canada), 90 Eglinton Avenue East, Suite 700, Toronto, Ontario,
Canada M4P 2Y3
(a division of Pearson Penguin Canada Inc.)
Penguin Books Ltd, 80 Strand, London WC2R 0RL, England
Penguin Ireland, 25 St Stephen's Green, Dublin 2, Ireland
(a division of Penguin Books Ltd)
Penguin Group (Australia), 250 Camberwell Road, Camberwell, Victoria 3124, Australia
(a division of Pearson Australia Group Pty Ltd)
Penguin Books India Pvt Ltd, 11 Community Centre, Panchsheel Park,
New Delhi - 110 017, India
Penguin Group (NZ), Cnr Airborne and Rosedale Roads, Albany, Auckland 1310,
New Zealand
(a division of Pearson New Zealand Ltd)
Penguin Books (South Africa) (Pty) Ltd, 24 Sturdee Avenue, Rosebank,
Johannesburg 2196, South Africa

Penguin Books Ltd, Registered Offices:
80 Strand, London WC2R 0RL, England

Published by Grosset & Dunlap, a division of Penguin Young Readers Group,
345 Hudson Street, New York, New York 10014. GROSSET & DUNLAP is a trademark
of Penguin Group (USA) Inc. Printed in the U.S.A.

Library of Congress Cataloging-in-Publication data is available.

ISBN 978-0-448-44431-4   10 9 8 7 6 5 4 3 2 1

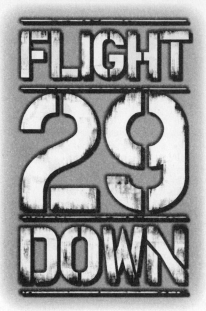

On Fire

A novelization by
Walter Sorrells

Adapted from the
teleplays by D.J. MacHale
Based on the
TV series created by
D.J. MacHale
Stan Rogow

Stan Rogow Productions · Grosset & Dunlap

PROLOGUE

It was just starting to get dark as Daley Marin stepped out of the girls' tent. She was planning on going into the woods where it was darker, so she had brought the lantern. She flipped the switch but nothing happened.

One of the flashlights had a bad connection already. And now this? Pretty soon they'd be out of lights.

She slapped the side of the lantern with her palm, hoping to get the light to come on. But it didn't. In the gathering gloom she noticed her ten-year-old brother, Lex, smacking the side of his flashlight over by the shelter where the boys were sleeping. His wasn't coming on, either.

"What's with the lights?" she said. "Was there some kind of atmospheric disturbance?"

"I wish," Lex said.

"Why? What happened?"

"I think the batteries are dead."

"No way!" Daley said. "Taylor's been keeping them charged . . . hasn't she?"

Lex rolled his eyes and shrugged.

"Where is she?" Daley said sharply.

Lex pointed toward a trail leading off to the beach. Daley immediately began marching in the direction he had pointed. Lex followed.

They had crash-landed—a plane full of teenagers—on a tiny island in the middle of the Pacific Ocean. The pilot and three others had left them to seek help, so it was just seven kids, all alone. Daley was furious. They couldn't afford to do stupid things like forget to charge the batteries! Food, shelter, light, fire—their lives would become incredibly hard and dangerous without these things. Daley had come to realize that it was her exclusive role in the little camp to protect these four precious items. Because if she didn't . . . nobody else would.

A few dozen yards down the trail, Daley saw Taylor Hagan hunched over a coconut candle, her long blond hair swaying in the soft breeze from the ocean. Apparently the wick was too short, because she was flicking the lighter over and over trying to get it started. But the lighter wouldn't spark. They'd already lost one lighter— smashed accidentally by Nathan thanks to one of Eric's thoughtless schemes to get out of work.

Luckily, Jackson had produced another one from his backpack, though he'd let the group worry for almost a full day before doing so.

This is not good, Daley thought, watching Taylor. The lighter was their only source of fire. If it burned out . . . well, Daley didn't even want to think about that.

"Taylor!" Daley barked.

Taylor made the usual wincing face that she always displayed when Daley talked to her. "I know, I know," Taylor said. "You don't have to say it. I let the batteries run down. My fault. I was busy."

"Busy? Busy doing what?" Daley demanded. "Taylor, you've only got one responsibility. *One.* And you can't even . . ."

"Please don't get all righteous on me," Taylor said. "It's no biggie. I'll charge the batteries tomorrow."

"And what about tonight?"

Taylor smiled smugly. "Oh, no problem. Observe."

She stood and walked down the trail toward the fire pit. Daley and Lex followed her.

"As soon as I realized that I'd forgotten to charge the batteries," Taylor said, "I knew we'd need light. So, *ta-daaaa!*"

Taylor waved her arm at a long row of coconut shells lined up along the side of the fire pit, each one containing a candle.

"We'll be fine for tonight. There's one for each of us, and more to spare."

"Hey," Daley said, "that was pretty smart."

"Thank you." Taylor shook the lighter. "Only ... now the lighter won't work. I think it's broken."

Daley and Lex looked at each other.

"Uh ..." Lex said. "How did you light all those candles?"

"Well, duh—with the lighter. It worked just fine until the last one."

"Wait. Are you saying you lit each one with the lighter?" Lex said. "You used it over and over? You didn't light one candle and then light the rest from that one?"

"That would have been a pain!" Taylor said dismissively.

Lex took the lighter from her and shook it. "It's not broken, it's out of fuel. You used it all up."

"Congratulations, Taylor," Daley said. "Nice job."

"Oh, man," Taylor said nervously. She looked at all the candles. "But ... it's no biggie, right? I mean, what about all the fuel we took from the plane?"

"Wrong kind of fuel, Taylor," Lex said. He held up the lighter and flicked it several times. "The flint's shot, too. It's totally done for."

Daley had about had it with Taylor's thoughtlessness. How many times had she made this kind of lame-brained move? "I don't believe it," Daley said, shaking her head.

"It's okay, it's okay," Taylor said—half nervous, half blustering. "We still have fire. The candles are lit. As long as we keep the fire going, we can always light up the next day."

"Sure," Daley said. "Until it rains."

They stood for a moment glaring at each other.

"Well," Taylor said. "We can cross that bridge when—"

She was interrupted by a peal of thunder. The three kids looked out over the darkening ocean. Not far away, a bank of thunderclouds was racing across the sky.

"Go on," Daley said, her voice full of mock innocence. "I'm listening."

Taylor continued to stare out at the onrushing storm.

"Oh boy," she said softly.

ONE

"**O**kay, check this out!" Eric said, focusing the reflector on the piece of dry coconut husk he held in his hand. "Presto, *fire*!"

Lex stood over his shoulder, watching. "Presto?" he said dubiously.

They stood at the edge of the beach. It was a nice clear day, no clouds in the sky. The storm that had put out all of their fires the previous night was now just a distant memory. The sun was beating down on them like a hammer.

Eric had spent all morning making the reflector out of a thin piece of metal he'd found in the plane back before it had washed away, polishing it and bending it until he was sure it would work. It was the same idea as using a magnifying glass to focus light into a point until it got so hot you could set things on fire. Only this used a reflector instead of a lens. Problem was, it seemed to be doing nothing.

Maybe it was the angle. Eric put the husk on the sand and repositioned the reflector.

Nothing.

Taylor came over and watched, too. "Fire?" she said. "I don't see any fire."

Eric felt a burst of irritation. Everybody was standing over him now, putting him on the spot. "Dude, you're in my light!" he said to no one in particular.

"Strictly speaking," Lex said, "I don't think that's the case."

"Well . . ." Eric grunted in frustration. "Well . . . well, anyway, you're crowding me," he said. "It's pretty much the same thing!"

He fussed with the reflector, bent it a little, polished it with his shirt. He had been totally sure this would work. But now he couldn't seem to get the thing to focus. All he got was this sort of jagged-looking blob of sunlight about the size of his fist. When he put his hand in front of the focal point, it got very warm. But it sure wasn't going to make anything burst into flame.

He had tried it earlier and gotten a brief puff of smoke. Surely if he could get a puff of smoke, he could get a fire. Right? What was going on?

Melissa joined the group. "Hey, cool," Melissa said. "Is that some kind of mirror for starting a fire?"

"Yeah, I'm still, uh, perfecting it," Eric said.

"That's kind of an understatement," Taylor said.

"I swear this worked before. The fire started, like ... fast!" Which was an exaggeration. But still ... at least it had done *something*.

"You know, there was a famous Greek mathematician, Archimedes," Lex said, "who built a weapon this way. They polished up these copper reflectors and then positioned hundreds of them on the shoreline of the city they were defending. It was so powerful that Archimedes could make entire ships burst into flame." Lex gestured, throwing a shadow with his hand. This time he really *was* blocking the sun.

"Thank you a totally *huge* bunch for that fascinating history lesson," Eric said. "But could you get out of my light?"

"I still don't think it's going to work," Lex said, moving his hand out of the way. "There's a problem with your focal length. See, what you need is a precise parabolic curve *here*, so that when the parallel rays of the sun come down *here*, they refract at a variable angle such that—"

"Okay, okay, whatever," Eric said. It was obvious that the stupid thing wasn't going to work. He picked up the reflector and heaved it angrily across the sand.

Nathan came out of the trees carrying a stack of firewood. "Jackson and I have been cutting wood like crazy," he said, dumping the wood next to the ring of stones where they used to build their fires. "Now all we need is a decent way of starting a fire and we'll be all set."

Nathan walked over toward the group of kids, then looked down at the piece of metal. "Huh," he said. "We might be able to make this into a reflector and start a fire with it." He picked it up and looked at it for a minute, then threw it back on the sand. "Nah, I take it back, that piece of junk would never start a fire." He looked over at the group. "What are you guys doing?"

Eric was getting ready to stomp away when he noticed Jackson staggering and weaving out of the trees carrying a load of firewood. He was carrying a lot of wood, but not *that* much. Jackson was a pretty strong guy. No reason for that much wood to make him walk all crooked like that.

For a second Eric thought Jackson was just messing around. Everybody in the camp seemed to have a favorite Eric imitation now. *Oh, my spine!* they'd say, and they'd clutch their backs and everybody would crack up, making fun of the fact that he happened to be in very fragile physical condition. Hardy-har-har, a bunch of freakin' comedians. Eric was already working on a stinging comeback to Jackson's big joke . . . when he noticed how pale Jackson looked. And how his eyes didn't seem to be focusing right.

"Jackson?" Melissa said.

Jackson looked vaguely at the group. He almost seemed not to recognize them.

"Jackson . . . are you okay?"

Jackson nodded. Then he slowly fell forward on his face. The wood he'd been carrying spilled all over the ground—the biggest piece in his hand, of course, falling right smack on the reflector, destroying every bit of Eric's hard work.

After he fell, Jackson lay there in the hot sand, motionless.

For a moment everybody just stared.

Then Melissa squealed: "Somebody! Help him!"

Taylor and Melissa ran over to Jackson, both of them trampling over the reflector.

"Thanks," Eric muttered. "Thanks for all the support, everybody."

TWO

Melissa grabbed Jackson's arm and helped him up into a sitting position. The skin on his arms seemed strangely hot. Taylor took his other arm, supporting him so he wouldn't fall over.

"Are you okay?" Taylor said.

"What's wrong?" Melissa added.

Jackson's voice came out weak and indistinct. "I don't know. I've been feeling weird all morning. My gut's in a knot. I got all dizzy, then when I was walking back to camp I puked."

Melissa felt his forehead. It was burning up. "I think you've got a fever."

Jackson pulled his arms into his chest and hunched over in a ball. "Man, I'm freezing!"

"Definitely fever," Melissa said.

"We better get him back to the shelter," Taylor said, "so he can lie down."

Melissa

So it's finally happened, the thing we've all been worrying about. One of us got sick. It's Jackson. He's shivering and throwing up and stuff. Nobody knows what's wrong. If it was food poisoning, you'd think we would have all gotten sick.

It's weird—when you get a fever at home, you just feel like, *Okay, it's a free pass. No school.*

But here? Here, it's really scary. No doctors, no medicine except for a little first-aid kit. Some little bug that would come and go at home . . . well, out here it could kill you! I've been sitting here all morning with Jackson, and he just seems to be getting worse and worse.

I've never felt quite so alone or quite so stranded.

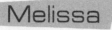

Jackson lay in the shelter, curled up inside his sleeping bag. Despite the suffocating heat, he was shivering almost uncontrollably.

Melissa and Taylor sat near his feet. They'd been trying to keep fluids in him, but it was a losing battle. And they were starting to run low on water.

They had stored a bunch of boiled water before Eric broke the lighter. But now several days had gone by and the boiled water was starting to run out.

Suddenly Jackson sat up, clutching his stomach. "I'm losing it," he whispered.

Taylor said, "You mean like . . ."

Jackson struggled feebly out of the sleeping bag. "Yeah."

He hobbled rapidly out of the shelter and headed down the path to the latrine.

"*Eeyew!*" Taylor said.

"Poor guy," Melissa said.

They watched him disappear into the bushes.

"What do you think's wrong with him? Do you think it's contagious?" Taylor asked.

Melissa shrugged. "Maybe."

Taylor's eyes widened and her face went white. She jumped up. "I just remembered, I need to, uh, talk to Daley about something."

She covered her mouth and walked out of the tent. Then suddenly she stopped and turned toward Melissa. "He's gonna be okay . . . isn't he?"

Melissa didn't answer.

Daley poured the last of the boiled water from the big plastic jug into the last of the bottles, then finished counting them. ". . . twenty-one, twenty-two, twenty-three."

"Twenty-three what?" Nathan said.

"Bottles of boiled water."

"That's not good," Nathan said. "Once we start drinking unboiled water, we're liable to get whatever Jackson's got."

"Well, I'm sure he didn't drink any unboiled water."

"No, of course not. He's not stupid. He knows there're all kinds of funky bacteria in it."

"And parasites."

"And diseases." They were silent for a moment.

"I'm just saying," Nathan said, "we need to get that fire started. Soon."

Daley moved the water into the cooler, then put it in the shade of the airplane wing. "We've got about two days' worth. If we really conserve water."

They looked at each other for another long moment. Technically, Taylor had been elected leader. But if stakes were raising again, Daley and Nathan couldn't just sit back and wait for her to take action.

"Time for a meeting!" they said together.

THREE

"The reason we called this meeting," Daley said, "is that we've got a serious problem. We've got about two days' worth of water. If we don't get a fire lit, then we're going to have to start drinking unboiled water. And that's not a good thing."

"No duh," Eric said.

"Could we try being constructive," Nathan said, "like just for two seconds?"

"Oh, excuse me," Eric said. "I spent all morning working on something to start a fire with and then everybody trampled it like a bunch of water buffalo."

"You have to admit it didn't work so great, though," Lex said.

"Okay, okay, hold on," Daley said. "What Nathan and I thought was maybe we could brainstorm a little. We'll come up with a bunch of possible ways to start a fire."

"No criticism or discussion of how we'll do it," Nathan said. "Just ideas. Then we'll assign each person to an idea. Surely if everybody takes an idea and runs with it, we'll find *one* that will actually work."

Eric held up his hand. "Okay, my idea is a reflector. I already worked on it. I got it to work once. But then something happened. I can't quite figure out what the problem is . . . but I know I can make it work."

"He's right," Lex said. "Maybe I could help him. There's an equation that would describe the curve that he'll need to create. Maybe if I worked on the math part for a while, he'd be able to improve the performance of—"

"No, no, no!" Eric said. "No math! Thank you, no, genius boy! No math. Thank you very much, but this is my idea."

"Hold on, hold on," Daley said. "Let's just come up with the ideas first. Then we'll start talking about who'll make them and all that stuff."

"As we all remember," Nathan said, "I tried to start a fire by scraping pieces of wood together. Now, I've been reading the book my great-grandfather wrote about his adventures as an explorer, and I think I missed some details before."

"Hey, I've got an idea!" Eric said. "Could we

let a day go by without hearing about your great-grandfather, the bold adventurer?"

Nathan glared at Eric. "Did I criticize your idea?"

"Hey, I've got an idea!" Taylor said. "A kite."

Everybody looked at her blankly.

"Yeah, a kite. Like Benjamin Franklin, right? We put up the kite, attach a key, wait for a storm, lightning strikes, and it starts a fire."

"Ooo-kayyy . . ." Nathan said.

"I don't mean to be negative," Daley said, "but remember when we tried to make a kite and it crashed?"

"I believe it was Nathan who crashed it," Eric said.

"Thanks, Eric," Nathan said, "but it was an accident."

Taylor said, "In this book I read about Benjamin Franklin, it said—"

"You actually read a *book*?" Eric said.

"I thought we were brainstorming," a weak voice said, "and saving all the criticism for later."

Everyone looked at Jackson. He had been lying silently up till that point.

"Good point," Daley said. "Idea number three, the Ben Franklin method."

"So what's next?" Nathan said.

"Glass," Lex said, holding up his hand.

"Glass?" Daley said.

"Yeah. We don't have a magnifying glass. But if

we could find some glass and grind it into a lens, we might be able to focus the light like you would with a magnifying glass. Then we could start a fire easily. I saw a really interesting show on the Discovery Channel about the history of optics. It showed this neat little device they used—"

"That sounds kind of complex," Nathan said. "What would you use to grind it with?"

"Brainstorming, we're brainstorming," Melissa reminded him.

"But if we start with a bunch of ideas that are too ambitious . . ." he said.

"Yeah," Lex said, "but lemme tell you about this little doodad. It'd be totally simple to make. All we'd need—"

Once again, all of the kids started chiming in with their opinions.

"Okay, okay, hold on!" Daley said. "Next idea."

"I've got a simple idea," Melissa said. "Wasn't there a battery on the plane? For starting the engine?"

Lex nodded.

"Maybe we could connect some wires to it and short it out. That would make a spark, wouldn't it?"

Heads nodded all around.

"More ideas?" Daley said.

"What about flint and steel?"

"There's no flint on the island."

"There's obsidian. That's kind of close to flint!"

"Yeah, but—"

"Okay, okay!" Daley waved her hands. "More ideas."

What followed were increasingly outlandish ideas—everything from digging down in hopes of finding volcanic magma under the island, to creating explosive hydrogen gas using the solar battery recharger, to trying to achieve spontaneous combustion with fuel from the wreck of 29 DWN.

Everybody jumped in—criticizing, throwing out suggestions, talking over one another. Since nobody in the group had actually made fire, they mostly focused on how people had made fire in books they'd read or shows they'd seen on TV.

Suddenly Jackson's voice interrupted the discussion. "Is there any more water?"

Melissa handed him a bottle. "Here you go."

Jackson took a sip and lay back on the sleeping bag. Then, just seconds later, he groaned and rolled up into a ball, clutching his stomach.

"I feel like somebody stabbed me in the stomach," he said.

"It's probably just gas," Melissa said.

"Nice," he said. "Just what I want everybody talking about . . . Jackson's gas."

The group laughed, then they went back to talking about ways of starting a fire again. Within minutes everyone was bickering and talking over one another again.

"Hey!"

It was Jackson again.

Everybody went silent. Jackson sat up slowly.

"Can I make a suggestion?" he said. "Everybody here is full of opinions. But none of us have ever successfully made a fire. I mean, other than with a lighter or a match. Right?"

There were nods all around.

"Everybody's talking about stuff they read about. Or something they saw on *MacGyver.* Or the History Channel. Or something their great-grandfather did. But the truth is—none of us knows squat."

There was a glum silence.

"I'm not saying this to be mean, okay?" he continued. "But you guys have been spoon-fed all your lives. There's always been a coach or a teacher or Mom or Dad standing there sticking their finger in an instruction book, going, 'Here, son, look at the instructions. Here's how it's done. Here's the correct and approved way.' "

"Well, how else are you supposed to learn anything?" Daley said.

Jackson looked thoughtful for a moment. "Do any of you *enjoy* school? I mean, I don't. Not really. I do my homework, mostly. I happen to be pretty good at schoolwork. But . . . *enjoy*? Nope. I'm just jumping through hoops so I won't end up living the kind of crappy life my mom's led. But there are a couple things in my life that I just love to do. Not because anybody's gonna give me a trophy, or because some rich dude in a necktie thinks it's all worthy and everything, or because it'll help me get into USC. Just because I dig it. You know?"

Blank expressions all around.

Then Melissa started to see what he was getting at. Or she *thought* she did. "You're saying that people will work harder on stuff they're passionate about."

Jackson nodded. "Harder, smarter, longer, faster."

Nathan squinted at him. "Okaayyy," he said. "But, uh, what's that got to do with starting a fire?"

"Here's my guess," Jackson said. "I bet everybody here has something that they love to do. They probably think it's all goofy and dorky and stuff. So it's, like, a total secret. But when you've got nothing you're 'supposed' to be doing and nobody's watching you, it's the one thing you'd choose to do. And you'd totally get into it. You'd do it harder and better than anything at school, than anything your parents want you to do . . ."

"Not really," Daley said. "I happen to like school."

Jackson gave her a long look. "What would you do if no one was looking?" he said finally.

"Like who?"

"Anybody," Jackson said. "Your friends. Your parents."

"Or like our teachers or coaches?" Nathan said.

"Exactly." Jackson kept looking intently at Daley.

After a second she looked away like she was embarrassed. Though Melissa had no idea what she might have been embarrassed about.

"For once, throw away the stupid instruction manual," Jackson said. "Find something that gets *you* on fire. Then use it to make a spark."

Everybody looked at him for a long time without responding.

Suddenly Jackson curled up in a ball and moaned.

"Jackson?" Melissa said.

Jackson climbed slowly to his feet and hobbled off toward the latrine.

Eric held his nose. "Man, you better believe *I'm* not going over there anytime soon."

They all stared at him expressionlessly.

"What!" he said.

"So . . ." Daley said. "Is it just me? I mean, Jackson's a pretty smart guy. But his idea seems kinda weird."

Nathan nodded wordlessly.

"Yeah," Taylor said. "That was like . . . wheeeww!" She made a chopping motion over the top of her blond hair. "Right over my head."

"Melissa?" Daley said.

"I . . . uh . . . I'm not totally sure I got it, either."

"Eric?"

"It's the fever," Eric said. "The guy's totally hallucinating."

"Okay then," Daley said. "So we'll go with our original plan. Eric, you'll perfect the reflector. Nathan, the method from your great-grandfather's book. Lex, flint and steel. Melissa . . ."

After they had finished parceling out the tasks, Daley stood up and said, "Okay, everybody. We've got two days. Then we're out of safe drinking water."

FOUR

"**A**nybody seen the camp knife?" Nathan asked.

Lex shook his head. "Not lately. The machete's over there, though," he said pointing over toward their collection of supplies.

"I've been looking all over for that camp knife," Nathan said. "It'd be a lot better for making my bow and drill than the machete."

"Sorry."

"No problem. I'll check with Daley." Nathan scanned the area, looking for the camp knife. "How's the flint-and-steel project coming?"

"I haven't really started."

"Okay, cool. Well, if you see that camp knife, let me know, huh?"

Lex nodded, then watched Nathan walk away.

Lex wished they'd assigned him to work on the

reflector instead of the flint and steel. He had what he thought would be some very helpful ideas for the reflector. But the flint-and-steel thing seemed less interesting. As far as he knew, you had to have the right kind of rocks. He remembered going camping a few years ago with his Cub Scout troop, and all the kids had tried to start a fire by banging rocks together. But nothing had happened.

Then one of the other boys' fathers had come over and struck sparks immediately. "Gotta have the right kind of steel and the right kind of rock," he'd said. "Otherwise, forget it."

At the time Lex had wanted to ask what the right kind of flint and the right kind of rock were. But he hadn't really had a chance.

Flint. What kind of rock was that? He wasn't totally sure, but it seemed like it would be igneous, right? Which came from volcanoes. This was a volcanic island. Therefore there should be some flint here, right?

He totally had no idea.

Lex sighed. Well, maybe if he wandered around and picked up all the rocks he could find, he could try them one by one until he found one that worked.

He walked down the path leading into the jungle. The path led past his garden. He checked on all the little shoots that were coming up and pulled a few weeds.

Everything was looking shipshape with the garden, so he decided to forge on into the jungle. Whew! It was already getting very hot. He swatted at a mosquito that landed on his arm. Another one landed on his neck.

He sighed and slapped his neck again, scanning the ground for rocks. This was not going to be very fun.

Rocks. Where could he find some good rocks? There seemed to be nothing on the ground here but sand. Hmm.

In the distance he could see the mountain rising up from the jungle. It was probably an old volcano. Maybe there would be some good rocks over in that direction. He began walking toward it.

Make hydrogen? Were they joking?

Taylor looked at the solar battery charger. It was a flat black square with a doodad that you could attach to a battery. After you left it in the sun for a while, the battery would be recharged.

Lex had said something about how if you put wires from what he called an "electrical source" into water, it would produce hydrogen. *Simple!* he had said.

Even if that was true—and it seemed ridiculous to begin with—how did you capture the hydrogen? And what would you do with it once you had it?

Totally dumb!

So, first things first. Water. Did it have to be *clean* water? Lex hadn't said. Better safe than sorry, right?

She took a bottle of drinking water and poured it into a bin she'd salvaged from the jungle that morning. Hmm. Didn't look like much. She took another bottle and poured it into the bin.

"What are you *doing*?" a voice behind her said.

Taylor whirled around. Daley, of course. Taylor said, "I'm making hydrogen."

"That's our drinking water!" As usual, Daley had seized the opportunity to rag on Taylor. What was her problem?

"Duh!"

"Why are you using drinking water for that?"

"Well, it needs to be clean water."

"Says who?"

Taylor scowled. "So . . . I guess you're an expert on making hydrogen?"

Daley just glared at her. "Water," she said. "Any kind of water can be used to make hydrogen. It doesn't have to be *clean*."

"And you know this because you've done it yourself?"

Daley scowled.

"Uh-*huh*!" Daley said.

Taylor turned her back on Daley. Daley kept standing there for a minute. Finally she stalked away.

Okay, Taylor thought. *So what else did Lex say?* You put wire from an electrical source in the water. The charger was an electrical source, right? So she'd need wires from that. She turned the charger around. There was a pair of wires sticking out from the back. She took out a pair of her nail clippers, clipped the wires off, and dropped them in the water.

She looked at the wires. They lay motionless underneath the water, two short curls, one red, one black. They didn't seem to be doing anything. But then, Lex had said it would take a while.

What else had he said? A collector. All she needed now was something to collect the hydrogen in. How did you collect hydrogen? She had no idea. Maybe with another bin? Maybe the hydrogen would sort of collect in the first bin. If she put that bin inside a second bin, the hydrogen would flow out into the bigger bin. Then more would collect.

She found another bin over by the girls' tent, brought it back, and set the small bin full of water into the larger bin.

Then she tried to remember what else Lex had said. That was pretty much it. Wire from the electrical source. Wires go in the water. Wait. Collect hydrogen.

Done! She was totally rockin'! Nothing to it.

Taylor looked up at the sun. Hmm. Might be time to lie down on the sand, work on her tan a little. She clapped her hands together in satisfaction and headed back to the tent to get her towel.

Eric was feeling a little bummed. His reflector looked like a piece of torn-up tinfoil. He was going to have to start from scratch.

He'd already spent hours on the stupid thing. Hours!

The idea of starting over made him exhausted. Maybe he needed to rest up a little.

Across the beach he saw Taylor working on the hydrogen-making thing. He still wasn't clear on the purpose of that. Best he could tell, the idea was to collect some hydrogen, make a spark by shorting out a battery, and *boom*, big flame. Sounded dumb to him. Like a good way to blow somebody's face off.

Well, maybe he'd go over and shoot the breeze with her a little. Anything to avoid actual work.

He searched around for his flip-flops. The sand was starting to get too hot to walk on. Oh, there they were.

By the time he'd gotten his flip-flops on, Taylor was gone. *Well,* he thought, *might as well go see what she's accomplished.*

He walked over and peered down at the stuff she'd been working on.

Two pieces of disconnected wire lay in a puddle of water in the bottom of a plastic container. So apparently she'd quit in the middle. Eric knew the wires had to be connected to a battery or something before you could produce hydrogen. Plus, they'd all learned in chemistry class that hydrogen was lighter than air. You'd have to put the big bin *over the top* of the small container. Otherwise—even if you produced hydrogen—the stuff would just float away.

Taylor came out of the treeline about fifty yards away, spread out her towel, and lay down. She had a big self-satisfied smile on her face.

Eric looked at the bin with the wires lying in it. Then at Taylor. Then at the bin. Then at Taylor.

No, he thought. *She didn't actually think she was finished.*

Even Taylor wasn't *that* dumb.

Nathan's great-grandfather had been this famous explorer. And he'd written a book about all his adventures, which Nathan had brought on the trip. The book was cool because not only did it tell about all these places he'd gone, but it also had all kinds of hints about survival skills. Where to pitch a tent during a snowstorm, how to find water in the desert, how to pack a mule . . . well, okay, so maybe those weren't all *that* useful . . .

But it had a bunch of stuff about starting fires, too. Page 231. Nathan pretty much had it memorized. But he figured he'd take another look. A couple of weeks ago he'd tried to start a fire by rubbing sticks together. But it hadn't worked out so well.

This time, though, he was going to do it. He'd show everybody. There had to be some kind of detail that he'd missed. Right?

He lay down on the platform of their shelter and stared at the picture, read over the words again.

In my travels I have observed many instances of the so-called "drill method" of starting fire employed. While I have seen a number of variations of this method used by Cheyenne and Sioux as well as several African tribes, the best fire-starters I have seen were Australian aborigines. The key to their method was the employment of the so-called Black Boy Tree (Xanthorrhoea). This soft, dry tree easily reduces to an incendiary powder, which ignites quickly and effectively. Absent a soft, dry tree of this type, the drill method will be mastered only with difficulty.

Moreover, in my experience this method works most effectively in hot, dry climes such as the upland plateau of British West Africa, where excessive atmospheric moisture does not spoil the fire-making potential of fallen timber. I have seen the method, on the other hand, produce mainly

*frustration when attempted in moist tropical locales.
During a hunting expedition in Dutch Guiana, for
instance ...*

Great. Somehow he'd missed the part that said only a moron would try this when they were marooned on a tropical island.

Still, Nathan had said he was going to make it work. So he'd make it work. Last time they'd tried rubbing the stick back and forth in a little trough in a piece of wood. This time he'd try a different approach.

There were nice clear pictures in the book of the so-called "bow-and-drill" method. First you made a sort of bow out of a stick and a piece of string. Then you took a hunk of wood and carved a small depression in it. Then you looped the bowstring around a short stick, stuck the bottom of the stick in the depression, and sawed the bow back and forth. The motion of the bowstring would rotate the drill rapidly, creating friction. Eventually it would create a tiny pile of hot coals out of wood dust shaved off from the stick. You stuck your tinder on the coals and blew gently.

And voilà! Fire.

Or that was the theory.

It looked simple enough. In retrospect it looked like it would work a lot better than the approach he'd tried before.

He looked around. String. Where could he find some string? Maybe from the ruined tent that had gotten blown away in the storm the other day. That would be perfect. Now where had they put it?

Daley would know.

"Daley!" he called. "Daley!"

Daley was walking toward the plane.

It was funny, really, thinking back on it. A few weeks ago they'd tried starting fires using all these primitive approaches, like rubbing sticks together. And it had been a waste of time. But the answer had been right there in front of them. Electricity. Take the leads off two batteries, stick them together, and they'd short out and make a spark. Not a *big* spark. But surely it would be enough.

And if it wasn't, worse came to worst, they'd make some hydrogen and put some tinder in a box with the hydrogen. Even a tiny spark would set off the hydrogen. Which would catch the tinder on fire. Nothing to it.

There was a battery in the plane. Thank goodness they'd managed to get some of the plane back out of the water.

She walked over to the remains of the plane and opened the little hatch on the nose cone, exposing a small battery—sort of like a car battery, but shaped differently.

Daley was dismayed to see that the terminals were all corroded.

"Oh, there you are," a voice said. She turned and saw Nathan walking across the sand toward her. "I was calling for you."

"What do you need?" she said.

"The tent that got torn up in the storm the other day? I need some of the nylon string from the rain fly."

"Oh, sure," she said. "It's in a bin underneath the shelter."

"Cool." Nathan looked over her shoulder. "What're you doing?"

"Salvaging this battery so I can create a spark."

"Looks pretty bad, huh?" Nathan said, looking at the white powder that covered both ends of the battery. "I bet it's dead."

"You think?"

"Sitting out there in the water?" he said. "It was out there for, what, three or four days? The electricity was shorting through the water the whole time. That's what all that corrosion is from."

"Shoot!" Daley said. "I didn't even think of that."

"What if we used the battery from the camcorder?"

"Taylor forgot to charge it."

Nathan rolled his eyes. "Figures. Well, I guess you can just use the charger itself." He frowned. "Wonder what she's planning on using to make hydrogen?"

They looked at each other. "Uh-oh!"

As she lay on the sand, Taylor's mind drifted. Finishing the hydrogen-making project had given her a moment of satisfaction. But now she just felt bored again.

Bored out of her skull.

Every day it was the same thing. Get up, get water, charge batteries, gather fruit, eat fruit, fish, eat fish, gather coconuts, eat coconuts ...

How long had they been here? Two weeks? Three? At first, living here had been terrifying. But now? Now every day was the same.

They needed something new, something exciting.

Suddenly she sat up straight. She had an idea. Genius!

Nathan and Daley found Eric lying on the sand. Taylor's towel was next to him. But Taylor was gone.

Nathan nudged Eric with his toe.

Eric sat up quickly, looked around, blinking. "What? Huh?"

"Please," Daley said sarcastically, "don't let us interrupt your beauty rest."

His eyes focused on Daley. Then he frowned. "Rest!" he said. "You thought I was *resting*? Dude, I was planning my improved reflector."

"Yeah, sure," Nathan said. "Where's Taylor?"

Eric shrugged. "She was right here."

"She didn't have the recharger with her, did she?" Daley said.

Eric scratched his head. "Yeah, I think she did. I think she was using it to make hydrogen. Though, I gotta tell you, I think she's in over her head on that project." He looked around, pointed at her towel. "Is that it under there?"

Nathan bent over and picked up the towel. Underneath was the square black solar panel.

"Excellent!" Daley said. "Now all I have to do is use the two wires coming out the back to make a spark."

Nathan turned over the solar panel and looked at the back. His eyes widened.

"What?" Daley said.

Mutely, Nathan turned the solar panel to face Daley. The wires had been clipped off cleanly right where they emerged from the recharger.

Daley felt a spasm of horror. Without the wires, the recharger was totally useless! Taylor had ruined it. Without the recharger, they had no batteries. Without the batteries, no camcorder, no flashlights . . . and no spark.

"Taylor!" Daley screamed. "Tay-*lor*!"

FIVE

Once he got out into the jungle, Lex realized that the mountain was a lot farther away than it looked. Every day he had been making a point to explore deeper into the jungle. By now he'd gone pretty far from camp.

Lex carried a day pack with him. Periodically he would search around for rocks. And when he found one that seemed interesting or different, he'd put it in the pack. He'd tried striking them against each other. But so far, no sparks.

No worries, though. There was probably a trick to it. He'd sort it out later.

Most of the older kids seemed to think the jungle was pretty creepy. And let's face it, there were lots of weird vines and huge bugs and stuff. But once you got used to it, the jungle was pretty cool. The main thing was that it was disorienting. Most of the time you couldn't see the mountain or the ocean. So unless you knew where you were, it was easy to start going in the wrong direction.

Lex wasn't worried, though. He had plenty of water, some dried fruit, and dried fish. Worse came to worst, he'd be fine. And at the end of the day it was easy to know which direction to go. All he'd have to do was follow the sun and it would take him right back to the ocean.

Plus, whenever he explored he made a point to break branches on the bushes every ten or twenty feet. If he got lost temporarily, all he had to do was start walking in an expanding circle until he found a broken branch; then he could follow the broken branches back to camp. That was the theory, anyway. So far he'd never actually gotten lost.

Ahead of him Lex heard a strange sound—almost like a cat. Only it came out of a tree. He stopped and listened. What a weird sound! Then he heard it again.

Could there be some kind of wildcat here? A cat that lived in the trees? He strained his eyes. The strange cry drifted down again. Suddenly a beautifully colored red and yellow bird exploded from the branches above.

It wasn't a cat; it was a bird! The bird flew a few hundred feet and landed in another tree. Without giving it any particular thought, Lex followed the bird, curious to get a closer look.

As he got closer, the bird turned toward him, appearing to study Lex with its large beady eyes. It was a big bird, bigger than a crow, with a long curved beak. The bird seemed annoyed at Lex's presence. It sort of harrumphed and strutted, making the feathers on its shoulders bristle.

Lex laughed. It was a comical bird.

The bird seemed annoyed by Lex's laugh. It gave him another long irritated stare, then flew off another few hundred feet. Lex followed.

The closer Lex got, the more agitated the bird seemed to get. It strutted and mewed and eyeballed him, sticking out its chest and puffing up its feathers.

"Sorry, pal," Lex said, "but you're just not scaring me."

The bird seemed to take offense at this. It spread its wings, flapped angrily, then flew off again.

And disappeared.

Lex looked around.

Oops. He'd been so interested in the bird that he'd forgotten to break branches.

Oh well, he was pretty sure he remembered the way back to where he'd started. He sat down for a minute with his back to the tree, pulled out his bottle of water, and took a long pull.

This was excellent. No big kids telling him what to do. Pretty soon he'd find some flint. Then when he came back, he'd start the fire and they'd have hot food again.

SIX

Jackson lay on the platform of the shelter. Melissa sat. She wanted to help, but it seemed like everything she did backfired.

"What is *wrong* with me?" Jackson said.

"I don't know. Can I get you something? What can I do to help?"

"Nothing," Jackson said.

Melissa thought back to one of the first times she had talked to Jackson back in school.

"Hi, Jackson!" she'd said.

"Hi." Jackson hadn't seemed all that friendly.

"Listen, I wanted to make sure you knew about the big trip. I'm on the planning committee. And since you're new, I thought you might not have heard."

"Where're you going?" Jackson asked, not sounding very interested. "A museum?"

Melissa had laughed. "No! It's an eco-camping trip to Palau."

"Palau? Sounds like something on a take-out menu."

Melissa had laughed again. "No, it's a beautiful tropical island in the Pacific, sort of near Guam. We're going to camp in the jungle for seven days. Isn't that awesome?"

For a moment there had seemed to be a spark of interest behind Jackson's usual facade of cool. But then he'd just shrugged. "Awesome? Yeah, I guess. And expensive."

"It's not that bad. We've had tons of fund-raisers so the campers only have to put up half."

"Half of nothing is still nothing. Which is pretty much all I've got."

"Oh. Well. Think about it."

"Thanks, but I think the only way I'll get to Palau is in my dreams."

"Maybe if your parents—"

"Parents?" Jackson's face had hardened slightly. "Don't exactly have any of those." Then he'd walked away.

What did he mean by that? she'd wondered.

Melissa still wasn't quite sure what Jackson's family situation was. She knew that his mom was in some kind of bad situation that had led to his going into foster care. And she'd never heard him even mention his father.

As she was thinking, she heard footsteps. Nathan and Daley.

"How's he doing?" Nathan said.

Melissa looked over and saw that Jackson appeared to have drifted off to sleep. "Not so well."

"We need to keep pumping water into him," Daley said.

"I'm trying," Melissa said. "But it all comes back out. If he's not throwing up, he's . . . you know . . ."

"Got it," Daley said. "Don't need details."

"If he doesn't stop, he's gonna dehydrate," Nathan added.

"It must be something he ate," Daley said.

"Yeah, but what?" Melissa said. "We all ate the same things. Dried fruit and dried fruit and dried fruit and fresh fruit and dried fruit."

"Don't forget dried fish," Daley said.

They stared at Jackson. His breathing was shallow and his skin was pale. There seemed to be nothing they could do.

"So, look, have you seen Taylor?" Nathan said to Melissa.

She shook her head. "Why?"

"Well, she just ruined the solar battery charger."

"You're *kidding*!" Melissa said.

"Cut the wires off the back," Nathan said. "I think maybe we need to just get rid of the hydrogen project. If we let her try anything else, there's no telling what she might destroy."

Melissa smiled wanly. At this exact moment, she wasn't all that concerned about the fire. She was more worried about Jackson.

"You think he's contagious?" Nathan said.

"Maybe," Melissa said.

Nathan and Daley looked at each other. "You know what?" Nathan said. "Maybe I ought to go find nylon cord so I can get started on the fire."

"Yeah," Daley said, "maybe there's a battery left in one of the flashlights that's still got enough juice left to make a spark."

Melissa watched them as they walked quickly away from the shelter. After they'd disappeared, she began to cry.

Jackson stirred slightly and opened his eyes. She tried to turn away so that he couldn't see her tears. But she didn't turn away in time.

"What's wrong?" Jackson said groggily.

Aside from the fact that you might dehydrate and die? Melissa thought.

"We're all alone here," Melissa said. "There're no doctors here, no hospitals, nobody to turn to."

"I'm gonna be fine," Jackson said. His voice was hoarse and tired.

"But the thing is . . ."

"What?"

"The thing is, it's all my fault!"

Jackson shook his head. "No it's not."

"It is! It's all my fault!"

Melissa began telling the story of what had happened, explaining to Jackson exactly how everything had gone wrong.

It had all started just a few weeks before the end of their sophomore year. The planning committee for the trip was meeting after school . . .

"Great news!" Abby Fujimoto announced. Abby was chairman of the committee. "Fund-raising for the trip has gone through the roof. We've raised way more than half of the total expense."

Everyone in the room cheered.

Nathan chimed in: "So does that make the trip cheaper for everybody?"

"It could," Abby said. "But once you divide it all up, it won't make that big a difference for each of us."

There was a mutter of disappointment.

Abby held up her hands and smiled. "However. There are some better options."

"Such as?" Taylor said.

"There's enough money to sponsor a Hartwell student who might not be able to afford the trip otherwise. It could be a great way to give something back to the school for putting this together."

Melissa's eyes widened. It had given her a thought.

Taylor, on the other hand, yawned loudly. "Yeah, that's real sweet and generous and everything. What's the other option?"

"We hired a small company to fly us from Guam to Palau on two planes. I don't want to say they're dinky planes. But we could possibly hire a more expensive company and charter one *bigger* plane instead of two smaller ones. It'd probably be a little more comfortable and a little faster."

Heads nodded around the room.

"The ultimate decision is up to the adult sponsors," Abby continued, "but as the student planning committee, we've got a say. What do you think?"

"Wait," Taylor said, "are you saying that this flight's going to be *un*comfortable? That was the plan? To take an *un*comfortable plane?"

"No, it's not like that—" Abby said.

"Seems like a no-brainer." Daley jumped in. "If there was somebody that wanted to go but couldn't, we'd have heard by now."

"Not necessarily!" Nathan said.

Nathan and Daley were in the middle of

their race for president of the class. Pretty much anything Daley said was bound to draw immediate disagreement from Nathan. And vice versa.

"Do *you* know of somebody who's just sitting around waiting to go?" Daley said hotly. "Hmm?"

Nathan stiffened. "Well . . . uh . . . there *could* be!"

"Plus—" Daley couldn't resist driving home her point. "Plus, why compromise safety?"

"It's not really about safety," Abby said. "I'm sure the flights will all be safe."

Taylor held up her hand. "Comfy plane! Comfy plane! Everybody for the comfy plane, hold up your hand!"

"Let's get real here!" Nathan said. "We're about to spend a week in a tropical location, sleeping on the ground in tiny little tents with spiders and leeches everywhere—"

"Spiders!" Taylor shrieked. "Leeches?"

"Well, not really leeches," Nathan said. "I'm just saying, if you're all about comfort, why go on this trip at all? It's not like we're gonna be lying on the beach sipping frozen drinks the whole time!"

Taylor looked around, blinking. "We're not?"

Everybody started talking over one another then, blurting out their opinions, nobody listening to anyone else.

Finally Daley waved her hands and shouted. "Okay, okay. I say we put it to a vote. Abby?"

Abby looked around the room. There was a brief silence.

Then Melissa held up one finger. "Um?" she said. "Can I say something?"

Abby nodded. "Sure, Melissa."

"Well, everybody's kind of making abstract arguments here," Melissa said.

"Huh?" Taylor said, squinting at her.

"Look, I know somebody who I think would like to come. Somebody that's had kind of a rough time. Somebody that definitely can't pay for the trip himself."

"Who?" Abby said.

"The new guy? Jackson? From what I've heard, he's been through some stuff. I know there have been rumors going around about him, about how he's been thrown out of a bunch of schools. But he wouldn't be here if he wasn't a bright guy, if he didn't deserve a chance. Guys, this could be his last stop."

A couple of heads nodded.

"I mean, look around you," Melissa continued. "Everybody here's got the latest electronic toys, the nicest clothes, their own car . . . This guy Jackson—I'm not even sure he has parents. We could be giving him the chance of a lifetime. So what if we have to fly in a smaller plane for a couple more hours? I mean, how selfish can we get?"

Melissa kind of surprised herself with her

conviction. She felt her face flush.

"Sorry," she said. "I got a little carried away."

The room was silent for a long time.

Finally Nathan said, "If he wants to go, I think we should sponsor him. Votes?" He held up his hand.

"Well," Daley said grudgingly, "it's against my principles to agree with Nathan, but . . ." Then she held up her hand.

Everybody laughed. Abby raised her hand. Then Jory Twist. Then Ian. Then several of the other kids.

Finally only Taylor was left. She blew a bubble with her bubblegum, then shrugged. "Hey, he is kinda cute," she said.

"So," Abby said, "it's unanimous. We'll ask Jackson if he wants to go."

Melissa finished her story. Only then did she notice Jackson was snoring.

She smiled a little. Well, at least maybe the sleep would help bring his strength back.

SEVEN

"It's coming," Daley said.

"What?" Nathan said.

Daley held up a piece of paper she'd just found in the bin where the water was stored. It was pink with red ink spelling out the words IT'S COMING in block capital letters.

"Weird," Nathan said. "I found one just like that over there where we put all the dried fruit." He held up a similar slip of paper. The only difference was that this one had the words IT'S ALMOST TIME! written on it.

Just then Eric approached. He was carrying his battered reflector along with the old ammo box he'd found a few days earlier.

"Wanna see something strange?" he said. Not waiting for a reply, he cracked open his ammo box and pulled out a piece of pink paper.

" 'It's nearly here,' " he read.

Nathan held up his paper. As did Daley.

"Well, that's bizarre," Eric said. "Wonder who put it there?"

"And *what's* coming?" Daley said.

"Yeah, what *is* coming?" Nathan said.

The three looked at one another. They all shrugged.

Lex wasn't exactly *worried* yet. He squinted up into the dark canopy of the jungle. No, worried wasn't the right word. Concerned? Nervous? Disconcerted?

Well, the point was, he was lost. Okay, there, he'd said it. *Lost!*

For a while he'd been fooling himself, trying to think of words that meant "lost" but that didn't sound like such a big deal. But the right word just hadn't come to him.

It was still more or less midday, the sun so high up in the sky that it was impossible to know which way was west or east, north or south. And he couldn't see the ocean or the mountain because of the trees.

He'd tried circling until he found some of the broken branches that he'd left to mark his trail earlier—only to discover that it was impossible to know if you were going in a circle when there were no reference points, no horizon, no straight lines, nothing but tree trunks and bushes and big spiderwebs.

He had been picking up rocks all afternoon, and now he was conscious of just how heavy the stupid backpack was getting. Sweat was dripping in his eyes, mosquitoes were biting him, sawlike blades of grass were cutting his legs, his back was sore . . .

And now the water was running out faster than he'd anticipated.

Bottom line? He was pretty sick of the jungle. He was ready to see the other kids. And especially Daley. She'd fuss over him, put some Band-Aids on his cuts, scold him for being out in the jungle for so long.

He hated to admit it, but it would be kind of nice.

Right now? Right now, he didn't give a hoot about making fire. He just wanted to get home.

Melissa watched Jackson sleep for a while. He seemed agitated, his eyes moving under his eyelids, his hands and feet jerking around like he was having bad dreams.

Eventually she noticed that the water bottle he'd been drinking from was empty. *Better go grab some more,* she thought.

He was shivering a little, so before she left she reached over and straightened his sleeping bag. As she did, she noticed a small piece of paper wedged under his pillow. She pulled it out and read it as she walked quickly down the trail to the tent: THE EXCITEMENT IS BUILDING!

What could that mean? she thought.

She reached the tent, where she found Eric, Daley, and Nathan clustered around Eric's ammo box.

"Anything else in there?" Daley said.

Eric shook his head. "Just the note."

They all looked up as they heard Melissa approaching. "You know anything about this?" Daley said, holding up a piece of pink paper. Then Nathan held one up, too. As did Eric.

Melissa reached into her pocket and pulled out the one she'd just found. "This one was under Jackson's pillow," she said.

They all looked at one another.

"Bizarre!" they said simultaneously.

Lex suddenly found himself running. He wasn't running *to* anything and he wasn't running *from* anything. He was just running. Pretty much panicking, actually.

He ran up hills and through swampy depressions, in and out of clearings and through places where the underbrush was so thick he couldn't see more than six or eight feet in any direction.

But he never saw the ocean or the mountain—or even more than a glimmer of the sky. The sun was barely penetrating the canopy of the trees high above him.

Finally he stopped running. This was getting him nowhere. He was so winded that he could barely catch his breath. He dropped his backpack full of rocks on the ground and slumped down onto the spongy jungle floor. His arms were covered with spiderwebs and his face was streaked with sweat and grime. He felt like crying. Suddenly he wanted his mother so bad.

He took a swig of water. Not much left. He decided he'd better start rationing it or he was liable to run out before he got back to camp.

After a minute, he started humming.

And when he started humming, that made him want to sing. He looked around furtively—as though there might be somebody in the jungle watching him.

Lex was embarrassed about singing. He didn't mind if people thought he was a boring science geek. But singing? Nah, singing was totally off the road map. He wouldn't sing around other people, not in a million years. It made him feel like a total dork.

But still . . .

There was nothing in his life that had ever been as comforting as singing. And since he was by himself out here in the jungle—hey, he could sing all he wanted! Just the thought of it made him feel better.

Lex would never have admitted it to anyone, but he'd gone through a stage a few years back when he'd been totally obsessed with the show *American Idol*. The year that his father and mother were getting divorced, Lex had watched every single show. Even the reruns.

But he didn't just watch. He also sang.

They had lived in a pretty big house, and midway through the year his dad had moved down to the basement. That year Lex's mom had stayed in her room all the time, doing yoga and playing all this horrible Indian music that sounded like somebody dropping a bag of spoons on the floor. And in the rare times his dad wasn't at work, he was holed up in the basement playing an electric guitar with his headphones on. So even though there were other people in the house, Lex might as well have been in an empty building. He was able to sing at the top of his lungs without anybody listening to him.

And dance.

And wear shirts unbuttoned down to his navel.

And pose with a microphone.

And put gel in his hair . . .

How many hours had he stood there in front of the mirror, singing? How many hours had he imagined the crowd cheering and chanting his name, the votes coming in over the phone, the dramatic moment at the end where they announced the winners for the week? Each week he would imagine the tension building. Then, finally, Simon Cowell going, "Well, Lex, I thought your performance was a bit derivative. But for someone your age? Totally astonishing." And then they'd announce his name! Yes! Moving on to the next round! Yes! Yes! Thank you!

His dad had all this recording equipment, so Lex had brought a bunch of it up to his own room. He stood there in front of the mirror dancing around and singing into the battered old Shure SM57 microphone until he could smell his breath on it whenever he picked it up.

Thinking back?

It was just plain weird.

But the funny thing was, he'd felt really happy when he was singing.

Maybe that's what Jackson had been talking about this morning. If you did something that made you feel good, then you'd do it really well. Not that Lex could see any connection between singing and starting fires. But what the heck.

Lex started singing at the top of his lungs. Back when he was totally into *American Idol*, he'd imagined the song that would win the contest for him. He'd thought a lot about it. It had to be an old song. You didn't get anywhere on *American Idol* singing new songs.

He'd settled on Elvis. "Heartbreak Hotel." *Wull since muh baby left muh. BUM BUM!* And then he would do this Elvis move with his hips in time to the drum part. *I founda new place ta dwell. BUM BUM!*

He had forgotten how good it felt. He hardly sang at all anymore. Not like when he was younger. And dancing? Forget it. He *never* danced anymore.

For the first few minutes that he sang in the jungle, Lex concentrated on his voice. But then he felt like he had to move, too. He spotted a stick on the ground—it was the exact same size as his trusty old SM57—picked it up, and started using it as a microphone. Doing all the hip-shaking stuff, too. Gesturing at the crowd with his arm, holding the "microphone" with his pinky finger sticking out, tossing his head ...

And before he knew it, Lex had almost forgotten that he was lost in a jungle on a flyspeck of an island in the middle of the ocean. He was in front of the *American Idol* audience, the judges looking at him, enraptured with his brilliant performance; the crowd going wild ...

Suddenly Lex noticed the bird again. The big red and yellow bird with the hook bill and the beady black eyes was staring down at him. For a second Lex felt ridiculous. Then he felt ridiculous for feeling ridiculous. It was a *bird*, for Pete's sake!

Who cared if a bird was watching him?

"Come on," Lex said, grinning and motioning to the bird. "Sing it with me on the chorus!"

The bird bristled and made a loud *caw*, then strutted up and down the branch, king of the tree.

Lex started singing "Heartbreak Hotel" again. The bird watched him intently as he sang about living at the end of Lonely Street and all that stuff. When he was done with the song, Lex struck a pose, then looked up at the bird. "Well?" he said. "What do you think? Am I the next American Idol?"

"Thank yeeewwww!" said the bird. "Thank yewww verrry much!"

Lex stared. The bird had just done an Elvis Presley imitation! Unless he was hallucinating. Which obviously he was.

"Did you just say what I thought you said?" Lex called to the bird.

The bird didn't answer. It just spread its wings, like it was taking a bow.

"Thank yeeewwww!" it croaked again. "Thank yewww verrry much!"

Then it flew away.

I am totally losing it! Lex thought. Then he tucked his "microphone" into his backpack and started hiking again.

E'GHT

Taylor was feeling good as she walked to the cluster of kids over by the girls' tent.

"So," she called innocently, "anybody know how you can tell if there's hydrogen in my machine?"

They turned toward her. For a moment their faces were blank.

Then Daley and Nathan's faces went stony.

"Machine?" Daley said.

"Are you being serious?" Nathan said.

Taylor blinked and looked from Nathan to Daley, then back to Nathan. "What?" she said. "I made the hydrogen thingy just like Lex explained it to me."

"So you did cut the wires off the back of the solar panel."

"That's what he said to do," she said. "Put the

wires from a power source into the water."

Nathan put his hands on his head and bowed over like somebody was dropping bricks on top of him. Daley rolled her eyes.

"What?" Taylor repeated.

Nathan sighed. "Okay, the point is, the wires have to be *connected* to the power source. Okay?"

Taylor felt a wave of irritation wash through her. "Well, why didn't somebody *say* so?"

"Um . . ." Daley said. "Maybe because only a total mental midget could possibly—"

"Okay, hold on, hold on," Nathan said. "Let's not go there. We've all discussed the issue and we've decided we can do without hydrogen."

Taylor looked around the group and then shrugged. "Whatever," she said. If they didn't want her hydrogen, that was their problem.

There was a brief, awkward moment, then Eric said, "You know anything about this?" He held up a slip of paper.

"It's a piece of paper," Taylor said, relieved to move on to another subject.

" 'The excitement is building'?" Eric said. " 'It's coming'?" He looked around the group. "What am I missing?"

"Whatever it is, we're all missing it," Daley said.

"This feels like Lex," Melissa said.

"Did you get one of these?" Daley said to Taylor.

Taylor made a strong effort to look innocent. She yawned and stretched. "Nope." She turned and started to walk away.

"Don't you want to know what it is?" Nathan called to her.

She stopped, looked back at them, and smirked. "I already know," she said.

Then she started walking again.

"Whoa, wait! *What's* coming?" Eric called.

"Maybe later," Taylor said.

NINE

Jackson looked up as Daley and Melissa climbed onto the platform of the shelter.

"You guys should stay back," Jackson said. He wasn't shivering now, but he had tried to stand up a couple of minutes ago and had barely been able to make it to the latrine and back.

"We're fine," Melissa said. "Besides, if it's contagious, I'm gonna get it anyway."

Daley and Melissa knelt in front of him.

"You know," Daley said, "we really need to figure out what you did differently than the rest of us. I just don't see how you would have caught it. There aren't any people on the island to have communicated the germs to you. And you can't catch the flu from a fish."

Jackson didn't really care. Truth was, he felt so crappy that nothing interested him. All he could think about was trying not puke all over himself. Or worse. "Go away," he said. "Let me sleep."

"Jackson, we brought you some more water," Melissa said. "You really need to drink or you're going to dehydrate."

"I can't keep it down. Beside, I'm so weak—"

"You think you're weak now?" Daley said. "If you can't start holding onto liquids, it's only gonna get worse until—"

Jackson felt like he was being tortured. "Okay, okay," he said. "What do you want to know?"

Daley, of course, had taken a bunch of notes. She ran her finger down the piece of paper, then cracked open the first-aid manual. "Okay. First question. Were you bitten by any bugs?"

"Only every day."

"Okay, but what about a strange bug?"

"Define strange."

"Be serious."

Jackson shrugged halfheartedly. "Far as I know, just the usual mosquito bites."

"See?" Daley said. "This isn't so bad."

Jackson didn't say anything. He was starting to feel cold again. He huddled deeper into the sleeping bag.

"Did you eat any bad fish?" Daley said.

"It all tastes bad to me," Jackson said.

"Are you washing your hands?"

"As much as anybody."

"What about fruit? Are you washing the fruit you eat?"

"I'm eating the same fruit as everybody else. If it's washed, then it's washed."

Melissa jumped in. "I wash the fruit in clean water before every meal."

Jackson said, "There you are, then."

Daley frowned and ran her finger down the list. "Bitten by monkeys?"

Jackson snorted.

"Stung by a jellyfish? Or a Portuguese man-of-war?"

"I think you'd have heard me scream," he said.

Daley was looking frustrated. "That pretty much leaves communicable diseases," she said. "Because obviously we're all drinking boiled water all the time. Right?"

Jackson looked at her without speaking.

Daley looked at Melissa, then back at Jackson. "Oh, come on! You didn't drink unboiled water! Did you?" Her eyes widened. "*Did* you?"

Once he'd found the yellow nylon cord that had been used to hold up the rain fly on the tent, Nathan had scoured the area looking for dry wood. From reading his great-grandfather's book, it looked like the key was to have a very dry wood that was soft enough to flake off as it was drilled. But not so soft that it would collapse or crumble when pressure was put on it.

There seemed to be a shortage of this kind of wood in the area.

Palm trees were too soft. Driftwood was too wet. Banana trees were too soft *and* too wet. When you went inland a little, there were big hardwood trees. But their wood was too hard and slick. It didn't seem like it would create much friction.

The whole enterprise was starting to get frustrating.

He decided to go ahead and make the bow. Without that, nothing else was possible. He cut a nice flexible piece of palm, notched the ends, and attached the nylon cord. Then he took a piece of hardwood that he'd found back in the jungle and hacked off a piece about the size of the palm of his hand. This would hold the top of the wooden drill. It was incredibly hard stuff, so it took forever to get the piece cut down to the right size.

When he was done, he dug a small hole in the wood for the drill to rotate in.

By the time he was done, it was late in the afternoon. Now all he needed were the two most important parts: the drill and the bottom piece. Now it was time for the soft, dry wood.

Daley walked up and said, "How's it coming?"

"Why can't we have crashed on the highland plateau of British East Africa?" he said.

"I didn't think there was such a place anymore."

"There isn't." He held up the two pieces of wood he'd been working on. "I've got the bow and the drill holder. But now I need the drill and the bottom piece. And they're supposed to be made from a kind of wood that seems to be impossible to find on this island."

"Maybe you could get Lex to help you," Daley said. "He's explored more of the jungle than any of us."

"That's a great idea," Nathan said. He looked around and frowned. "Where *is* Lex, anyway? I haven't seen him all afternoon."

"Really?" Daley narrowed her eyes and looked around. "Come to think of it, neither have I."

Nathan could tell she was worried. "He's probably just out there messing with his garden," he said.

"All afternoon?" she said.

"Give it another hour or two," Nathan said. "If he's not back by then, we'll go looking for him. I wouldn't worry."

"Yeah," she said doubtfully. "I guess you're right."

As they were talking, Melissa approached them.

"We've got a problem," she said.

"Only one?" Daley said.

Melissa smiled obligingly. "Well. It's the books. Everybody left their books on the plane. And now they're all soaked."

"Sure," Daley said. "Weren't you trying to dry them out?"

"Yeah, the problem is, the pages are all sticking together."

Daley looked puzzled. "Okay . . ."

"I'm trying to figure out if there's something we can do to make Jackson better. We've got the little first-aid booklet. But there's a better book that Abby brought. It's called *Jungle Medicine* or something like that. It's a lot bigger and has a lot more information than the first-aid booklet. Problem is, the pages are sticking together as it dries."

Daley looked at Nathan. "You go on," he said. "I'm gonna keep looking for some wood for my bow-and-drill fire-starter."

Daley and Melissa walked silently down to the beach where Daley found that Melissa had laid out several dozen books in a long row. They were all splayed open. In some cases the pages fluttered freely in the breeze. But in others, the pages were so gummed together they might as well have been blocks of wood.

"Here it is," Melissa said, picking up a large hardbound book. She handed it to Daley.

It was wet to the touch. Daley opened it slowly. The pages tore.

"Oops," she said.

"See what I mean?"

"Maybe if we're really gentle with it . . ." Daley said. She tried opening to the front of the book. It took her about a minute, peeling the page back with her fingernail. But even then it tore several times.

The page she'd turned to was the table of

contents. She scanned it to see if there was anything about waterborne diseases. Evidently the table of contents was several pages long, because all that was listed were joint problems and broken bones.

"Maybe if we leave it open to the table of contents," she said, "this part will dry in the sun. Then we can come back later and find what page would help us with Jackson."

"But that could take the rest of the day. Maybe even tomorrow."

Daley scratched her face. "Yeah, but if we destroy the book trying to find that page, it won't do us any good, either."

"Yeah," Melissa said. "I guess. I'm just so worried. I'm afraid if we can't make him better by tomorrow, he could be in real trouble."

"Let's give it a few hours," Daley said. She walked around looking at the books on the ground. Somehow during all her inventorying, she had missed some of these books.

One of the worst things about being on the island was that there was nothing to read. She picked up a thin paperback. On the front was a lurid picture of a woman in a flowing dress, her long red hair tangled and whipped by the wind. In the background was an English mansion. A muscular man wearing a nineteenth-century suit stood beside her, managing to look both adoring and menacing at the same time. It was called *The Maid of Westleydale Manor*.

Melissa pointed at the book and laughed. "Can you believe that?" she said. "There are at least five of those totally cheesy romance novels. Who in the world reads those things?"

Daley cleared her throat. "Who knows," she said vaguely.

She stared at the cover for a moment more. For some reason, the picture tugged at her. Finally she let go, dropping the book on the sand.

"Hey, be careful," Melissa said in a humorous tone of voice. "Another week here and I might be desperate enough to read that one, too."

Daley laughed.

Melissa's smile faded. "Look, I better get back and see how Jackson's doing."

"Sure," Daley said. "I'll, uh . . . stay here and see if I can't make some progress with the jungle medicine book."

Melissa nodded, then hurried off. Daley watched her go. Poor thing. She was totally infatuated with Jackson. And Jackson obviously didn't feel quite the same way. It was like something out of a romance novel.

Speaking of which . . . Daley thought.

She waited until Melissa was gone, then she looked around to see if anybody was looking. The coast was clear. She was completely alone on the beach.

A wave of excitement ran through her as she hurried over to the book she'd dropped on the ground, scooped it up, and stuck it under her shirt.

TEN

Down the beach a few hundred yards from the camp, Daley had found a large outcropping of volcanic rock that had been weathered and worn by the waves. In the middle of the outcropping was a small depression that had been hollowed out in such a way as to form a perfect seat.

The seat was sheltered by a palm tree, so it wasn't too hot. It had a back so that she could lean back and relax. The view was nice. Unbeatable.

Daley was not much for resting. But every now and then she wearied of the frantic activity that was her life. And when she did, she felt the urge to get away from everybody.

She felt guilty about leaving camp. There was so much to do. Jackson's illness and the fire-starting challenge had distracted them. But the fact was, just because somebody was sick and just because they needed to start a fire soon, that didn't mean the normal chores went away. Finding fruit, fishing, washing clothes, gathering nuts, airing out sleeping bags, sweeping the shelter—the list of things she ought to be doing went on and on.

She felt guilty enough about resting. But the truth was, she hadn't come here just to sit and stare at the waves.

She'd come here to indulge in her most secret and guilty pleasure.

Reading romance novels.

Back when her mom was dying of cancer, Daley had discovered romance novels. The kind she liked best were the cheapest, dumbest ones. Fiery English heroines from down-on-their-luck families who fell for obnoxious rich guys, mainly. Lord What's-his-name would always be this total jerk. But then in the end the determination and will of the fiery heroine would always subdue him and bring out his good qualities. And then they'd get married at the end.

She studied the soggy, warped cover of the book for a long time, the suave-looking guy with the ascot and the top hat staring at the red-haired girl. It filled her with a sense of excitement and relief. The thought of sinking into this world of carriages and vicarages and parlors and stilted conversation—it was such a relief, a shelter from the deluge of thoughts that normally bombarded her mind. In a romance novel, nobody had to clean up after the meal, nobody had to do homework, nobody had to take the SAT. And definitely, definitely, *definitely* nobody was marooned on some stupid little island where they had to engage in constant drudgery just so they wouldn't die of starvation.

Still . . . it was so embarrassing! Everybody on the island would die laughing if they knew she was into romance novels.

She read the first line of the book—and suddenly she started to relax. The pressures, the chores, the fears, the homesickness . . . it all began to fade.

"Evangeline!"

Lord Bernard Kint, the fourth Earl of Blackthorn, strode through the front door of Pendleton Hall, his hunting boots spattered with mud, and handed his fowling piece to Gibson the butler.

"Evangeline!" Lord Bernard bellowed again. "Where are you, you silly girl?"

Daley felt her entire body relax.

Thank you, God, she thought. *Thank you for romance novels!*

The bottle was empty.

Lex held it up in the air over his mouth. One last drop of water caught a thin shaft of light and glistened momentarily. Then it fell, missing his mouth.

This is not good, he thought. *This is not good at all.*

The good news was, even if he got stuck out here, he wouldn't actually die of thirst. He'd passed a small stream earlier in the afternoon. Well, he'd actually passed it about three times. Despite all his best efforts, he seemed to be going in circles. But still, he was kind of paranoid about drinking unboiled water. No point in drinking out of the stream until he was completely parched.

It was getting later in the day, and the air was cooling.

Now that the sun was lower in the sky, it was easier to navigate. The sun was over *that* way, so the camp had to be over *this* way. Simple.

He felt better now. Even if he was out of water, now that he was oriented, all he had to do was head south and eventually he'd hit the shore. If everything went perfectly, he'd run smack into camp.

If not, he'd just follow the beach until he found Daley and the others.

Nothing to it. Right?

He began walking again.

He was exhausted, though. His feet hurt. He could tell that he had blisters all over them. And the muscles in his legs hurt, too. And the backpack full of rocks? Forget about it. The straps were digging into his thin shoulders. And the rocks seemed to weigh more with each step he took. But he was on a mission. One of those rocks might be the one that would start the fire. He couldn't just throw them away.

He trudged on, knocking spiderwebs out of his way with a stick. He'd been walking steadily since midday. What was it now—five o'clock? Six? In six hours you could walk five miles. With all the walking in circles that he'd done, he certainly wasn't that far from camp. But he might be far enough that he wouldn't make it back by nightfall.

The idea of sleeping out in the jungle, especially with no water—he had to admit, it creeped him out. He began to walk faster.

Suddenly he saw something in front of him. A dark flash of something in the trees, accompanied by a loud clatter of wood.

What in the world was that?

Daley and Nathan had had a confrontation with a pig a few weeks ago. A huge, hairy boar with nasty curved tusks. Could that have been what he just saw?

He adjusted his course, veering a little more east. Pigs wouldn't attack you. But if you cornered one, spooked it, got between a sow and its young? Hey, a pig could hurt you, no joke.

How much farther? he kept thinking. *How much farther?*

He felt himself getting a little light-headed. The

sun was getting lower in the sky. There was another noise. It seemed to be coming right toward him.

Lex felt his heart begin to race. *What is it?*

He whirled.

There was a thrumming noise, then a flash of red.

It was the crazy Elvis bird again! Lex felt like he was about to faint with relief.

"You crazy bird, don't *do* that to me!" Lex said. "You about scared me to death."

The bird settled onto a branch about ten feet away from Lex and studied him with its beady black eyes.

"What?" Lex said.

The bird just kept looking at him.

Lex decided it was time for another break. Out of habit he took out his water bottle, only to feel a sudden sense of dismay when he remembered it was empty. Did he still have some food? He fished around in the side pocket of his pack. Inside were several pieces of dried coconut.

As he popped one into his mouth, the red bird flew down and landed on the ground just a few feet away. It continued to stare fixedly at Lex.

Lex took out another piece of coconut. "What?" Lex said.

The bird strutted over, craned its neck, and grabbed the coconut from his fingers. Before Lex could do anything about it, the bird had gobbled up the coconut.

"Hey!" Lex yelled. "That wasn't very nice."

"Thank yeeew!" the bird said. "Thank yeewww verrry muuucch!"

"Well, at least somebody taught you some manners," Lex said, laughing.

The red bird flew about ten feet, landed on a branch, and strutted up and down, looking very proud of itself for having made off with his food.

"Viva Las Vegas!" the bird said. "Thank yewww!"

"Okay," Lex said. "This is getting crazy."

Nathan was getting frustrated.

He'd found a bottom piece and drill. Now he was sawing back and forth. But the bow kept slipping and the drill would stick.

"Maybe you're holding it too hard," Eric said.

Nathan gave Eric a hard look. "Don't you have a reflector to make?"

"Hey, I'm just saying. Seems like you're leaning on it a little too hard."

Nathan held up the bow and the drill. "Here. Show me how it's done."

"No, no, no," Eric said, holding up his hand. "You're doing great." He made no move to do anything. As far as Nathan could tell, Eric had made no progress on the reflector at all. He'd kind of flattened it out a little to get the dents out from when it had gotten smashed up that morning. But that was about it.

Nathan reassembled the drill and started sawing away again. This time he held it more lightly. Still the drill kept jamming.

"What if you lubricated the top piece so it would spin easier?" Eric said.

"It's *fine*," Nathan said.

"Dude, it's jamming!" Eric said. "You need to put something in there that will make it smoother."

Nathan was getting pretty sick of Eric's peanut-gallery routine. "Such as?"

"Uh . . ." Eric blinked. Naturally he hadn't thought that far ahead. "What about grease?"

"Yeah, well, we're a little short of axle grease around here."

"What about, like, fish grease? You know those pink fish, when you cook them, there's some grease that oozes out?"

The muscles in Nathan's shoulder were starting to burn. He turned and looked at Eric. "You might recall," he said sarcastically, "that the whole reason I'm freakin' killing myself over here is because we don't have a freakin' fire to freakin' cook a freakin' fish on."

"Hmm," Eric said. "That's a good point."

Nathan tried a few more strokes.

"What about pencil lead?" Eric said. "Powdered graphite? Don't they use that to lubricate—"

Nathan threw the bow at Eric's face. It missed and landed in the bushes.

"Hey," Eric said lightly. "Just trying to help."

Nathan flopped back on the sand, knocking his backbone on a sandspur. "Ow!" He sat up and watched in silent fury as Eric ambled off. "Graphite," he muttered. "What a stupid idea."

After Eric was gone, Nathan stood up and retrieved the bow. He sat back down and sawed away for a while. It jammed after about five strokes.

Nathan was beside himself with frustration. They needed fire! They had to have it! With all the batteries in the camp exhausted, the charger ruined, and Eric's reflector looking like it would never be functional, all the burden was on Nathan. He *had* to make it work.

But how?

After a minute he sighed loudly and stood up to make sure Eric wasn't watching. Then he reached inside his pocket, found a pencil, and pulled it out.

Then he used his pocketknife to shave off a bunch of the graphite, making a tiny pile in the depression of the drill holder. Then he put the upper tip of the drill into it and smushed it around until he'd crushed the graphite into a fine powder.

"This'll never work," he mumbled. "I don't even know why I'm bothering."

Next he reassembled the bow and drill and took a tentative pull on the bow. He raised one eyebrow. Hmm! It actually did feel a little smoother.

He sawed tentatively a few more times. Still turning fine. He put a little more pressure on the drill holder and quickly yanked the bow back and forth.

Unbelievable! It was turning nice and smoothly. Graphite—who'da thunk it!

He began sawing away again, his spirits immediately rising. Smooth as silk. Now that was more like it!

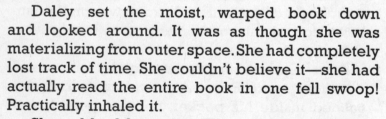

Daley set the moist, warped book down and looked around. It was as though she was materializing from outer space. She had completely lost track of time. She couldn't believe it—she had actually read the entire book in one fell swoop! Practically inhaled it.

She rubbed her eyes. The sun was starting to get low on the horizon.

Suddenly a tiny feeling of anxiety invaded her mind. Two hours had gone by and she'd accomplished nothing. She felt a moment of self-reproach. *This place will totally fall apart if I don't stay focused!*

She tucked the book under her shirt, then began walking quickly back to camp. As she walked, something else struck her. While she'd been sitting there reading that dumb book—well, it had actually been a pretty good one—self-indulgently wasting time, she hadn't given a single thought to Lex.

Where was he?

"Lex!" she called as she approached the camp. "Hey, Lex, where are you?"

Melissa looked up from the shelter. She was obviously still on her vigil with Jackson.

"Have you seen Lex?"

Melissa shook her head. "That jungle medicine book is starting to dry out, though," she said. "I think that we can—"

"Hold on," Daley said. "I gotta find Lex."

Taylor ambled by, heading in the direction of the beach. She was wearing sunglasses and a bathing suit and carrying a towel. Eric was following close on her heels.

"Have you seen Lex?" Daley called.

Taylor shook her head. "I'm going swimming," she said. "Wanna take a dip?"

"I need to find Lex first."

"Haven't seen him since lunch," Eric said.

"Lex!" Daley called. "Hey, Lex!"

There was no answer.

She left Eric and Taylor behind and headed over to the tent.

She found Nathan fiddling around with his bow and drill.

"Have you seen Lex?" she called.

"Hey, check this out," Nathan said. "I haven't actually got fire yet but—" Suddenly he frowned, as though what she'd said had only just penetrated. "You know, I haven't seen him since . . ." He looked at his watch. "Whoa. It's getting late."

"He went off to find rocks six hours ago. He's never been gone that long before."

Nathan looked concerned. He set down his bow and stood up. "I don't want to start freaking out or anything, but . . ."

His voice faded into silence.

He met Daley's gaze. She could tell that he was as concerned as she was. And that scared her.

"Oh, God!" she said. A stupid romance novel! She felt like the biggest jerk in the world. Lex was out there lost in the jungle—suddenly her mind started thinking of other more terrible alternatives—and she'd been reading a stupid romance novel. She put her hands over her mouth.

The romance novel fell out from under her shirt onto the ground. Nathan didn't seem to notice.

"Stay here," he said. "I'll get the others."

ELEVEN

"**L**ex! Lex!"

Everybody was yelling now, walking into the jungle in a line— just far enough apart that they could see the next one in line. The only person who wasn't participating was Jackson, for obvious reasons. Daley was feeling pretty scared now. Lex could be a little spacey, but disappearing into the jungle for five hours? No. Something was wrong. Hopefully he was just a little lost.

"Lex!"

There was no answer.

"Lex! Where are you? Lex!"

They were moving deeper and deeper into the jungle. They'd already left the line of palm trees along the shore, passed the clearing where Lex had planted his garden, and were now into thicker, more heavily forested territory. Some of the boys routinely wandered this far back into the jungle, but Daley had rarely come this far. She found it spooky. And there wasn't much in the way of food to be found here.

Strange birds screeched overhead, and the air seemed heavy and lifeless.

"Lex!"

"Hey, guys! Over here!" It was Nathan's distant voice, from the far end of the group.

Had he found Lex?

Daley ran toward the sound of Nathan's voice.

"What?" she said when she reached him.

He pointed at a small bush. A large lizard scampered away from them, disappearing under the bush with a clatter of leaves. She blinked. "A lizard?"

"No, here." Nathan pointed to a broken branch. "When Lex goes exploring in the jungle, he always breaks branches so that he can find his way back."

"How do you know he did that today?"

"It's fresh," he said. "See, you can see the sap coming out."

She leaned toward the broken branch. Nathan was right. Several small beads of sap glistened where the branch had been snapped off.

The others gathered around them.

"I say we follow the broken branches," Nathan said.

The group looked mutely at one another. "We've already gone a long way," Melissa said. "I'm a little worried about leaving Jackson by himself."

"Well, I'm a little worried about leaving a ten-year-old in the middle of jungle!" Daley snapped.

Melissa's eyes widened. "Sorry! I just—"

"Forget it," Daley said. She felt bad, but surely everybody would understand how worried she was.

Eric squinted off into the trees. The sunlight was slanting down through the foliage at a low angle. "You know, it's gonna be getting dark pretty soon," he said. "We better get some flashlights or we'll all be stuck out here."

"The flashlights are all dead," Daley said. "Thank you very much, Taylor."

Taylor rolled her eyes.

"What about that blue flashlight?" Melissa said. "Last time I checked, it was fine."

"I looked for it but I couldn't find it," Daley said.

"Well, it can't have just disappeared!" Taylor said.

"Look, Mel, why don't you go back and check on Jackson?" Nathan said. "If he's okay, then look for the blue flashlight."

Melissa looked relieved. "Okay."

She headed quickly back down the path toward camp.

"All right, let's keep moving," Daley said. "Anybody see another broken branch?"

When Melissa got back to the shelter, she found Jackson sitting up, looking out toward the ocean.

"How are you doing?" she said.

He shrugged weakly. "Where'd everybody go?" he said.

"We're looking for Lex."

"Oh," he said vaguely. Then he lay back down and closed his eyes.

Melissa took this as a bad sign. Jackson seemed to have a special bond with the younger boy. *He must be feeling seriously terrible if he doesn't even want to know what happened to Lex,* she thought.

"Can I do anything for you?"

Jackson didn't even stir.

She sat for a minute looking at him. Suddenly she remembered: *the flashlight!* She was supposed to find the blue flashlight.

She checked around the shelter, then over by the plane remains, then at the tent. The official policy—Daley's idea, of course!—was to store all the tools in the shelter and all electrical devices in the tent where they were least likely to get wet. But only Daley and Melissa were very responsible about putting things in their "official" storage areas. Everybody else seemed to just drop things wherever they were when they were finished using them.

Melissa scoured the camp but failed to find the flashlight. Odd.

While she was heading over to the beach, she took a detour to check on the medical book. The book was still pretty soggy. But the table of contents was dry. She flipped through it until she found: *Vomiting/Diarrhea, pp. 291-317*. You wouldn't have thought there'd be over twenty-five pages on a subject like that. But there it was.

She tried to open to page 291, but she only succeeded in tearing several of the preceding pages. When she was done, though, the book was open to a page fairly close to the ones she wanted to read. *At least I've got it open,* she thought. *Maybe those pages will dry overnight.*

By the time she was done messing with the book, the light was really starting to fade.

She took one last quick look around the camp. No blue flashlight. She checked all the other flashlights. All dead. As an afterthought—just in case one of them had a bad connection instead of a worn-out battery—she picked up each one and smacked it with her palm.

When she smacked the last one—the smallest of all their flashlights—it blinked on. Yes! It worked!

The light was a little dim. But it was better than nothing.

She sprinted off toward the tree line.

As Lex worked his way through the jungle, the terrain began to change. By now he was sure he'd never been on this part of the island. But the way the sun was slanting through the trees, he was sure this would get him to the coastline. Eventually.

The problem was that the hills were getting higher, the slopes steeper, and the ground slipperier. It was getting harder and harder to make progress.

He began to feel more and more worried. The only thing that kept him going was the big red parrot. It flew along with him, moving from tree to tree.

As he walked, Lex sang.

At first he'd tried different songs to keep his spirits up, singing them at the top of his lungs. But as the hills got steeper and steeper, and his throat grew more and more parched, he found that one song kept coming back. "Heartbreak Hotel."

Eventually he couldn't even sing the words. He just hummed, a rhythmic singsong that seemed to help him keep his feet moving.

"Hm-hm hm-hm hm-hmmm-hmmm, ha-huh ha-huh ha-huhhh-huhhhhh." Over and over.

Eventually it had pretty much stopped being a song. It was as if his brain and his mouth and his feet were all connected in one big rhythmic blur. *Find the ocean,* he kept telling himself. *Just find the ocean and everything will be fine.*

"Hm-hm hm-hm hm-hmmm-hmmm, ha-huh ha-huh ha-huhhh-huhhhhh."

The sky was getting darker and darker. But still he forged on. And still the bird kept up with him, fluttering from branch to branch. Every now and then he'd stop and feed some dried fruit to the bird.

His mouth was so dry now that he could barely chew the dried fruit himself. But he knew that as long as he kept feeding the bird, it would stay with him.

By now he was ready to drink anything—full of germs or not.

But on these high ridges he was climbing, there was nothing to drink. The trees were different now, too—smaller, thinner, drier-looking. His legs were getting rubbery now. At the top of one ridge he fell and almost rolled down the steep hill on the other side. His hand hit a thick stick. When he stood, he picked it up to use as a walking stick. Anything to steady his wobbly legs.

A fall on one of the steep hills, he thought vaguely, could be a serious problem.

He continued down the next hill, up the next ridge. He'd made it about halfway when he was suddenly overcome by gloom. It was close to full-dark now.

"I'm never gonna make it," he said to the red bird.

The bird looked at him with its black eyes.

"What?" Lex said. "Let's be honest. I'm not."

The bird just kept looking at him.

"Okay, *okay*," Lex said. "I'll go to the top of the next ridge. If I don't see the ocean, I'll just stop for a while. Actually, I'll stop for the night."

The bird puffed up its feathers. It looked like it was shrugging. Then it was airborne, flying up to the top of the ridge.

"What do you see?" Lex called wearily.

But the bird was gone.

Why am I even talking to a stupid bird? Lex thought. He pushed himself to his feet. The bag of rocks lay on the ground. For a moment he considered leaving it there. He just didn't have the strength to make it to the top. Not with a million pounds of stupid rocks. Rocks that weren't flint in the first place. Rocks that would never make a spark anyway.

But then he sighed, hoisted it onto his back, and kept climbing.

"Hm-hm hm-hm hm-hmmm-hmmm," he hummed. "Ha-huh ha-huh ha-huhhh-huhhhhh."

Above him, the ridge seemed to rise and rise and rise forever, a black shape against the ever-darkening blue-black of the sky. *I'm never gonna make it,* he thought.

TWELVE

"Lex!" Daley called. "Lex!"

"Seriously, Daley," Eric said. "I don't think Melissa's gonna find the flashlight. We need to head back or we're gonna get lost out here, too."

Daley looked at him furiously. "How do you know she's not gonna find it?"

"Uh . . ." Eric's mouth hung open for a minute. "I don't."

"Then shut your mouth."

"Hey, I don't *have* to help," he said. "Find the little brat yourself!"

"Yeah, Daley, and I'm sick and tired of raking spiderwebs out of my hair," Taylor chimed in.

Nathan held up his hands. "Guys, she's upset. Okay? Just chill."

"Chill!" Eric waved his hand in a big circle.

"Can you see anything out here? I can't see squat. All I see is a bunch of lumps and darkness and spooky-looking stuff. We won't be doing Lex any favors if we all get stuck out here."

Nathan sighed. Eric kind of had a point.

"Look, Daley," Nathan said. "If he's just lost, eventually he'll stop somewhere."

"What if you'd quit back when I fell down that hill?" Daley said. She was referring to an incident a few days earlier when she'd fallen down a ravine and almost gotten swept out to sea. If Nathan hadn't been persistent, she probably would have died.

"I know," Nathan said. "But how long's it been since we found a broken branch? Five minutes? We just can't see. Come on. Let's head back and we'll come out and find him in the morning. Hey, for all we know, he could be sitting back at camp right this minute."

Before Daley had a chance to reply, a distant voice yelled, "Guys? Daley? Hello?"

It was Melissa.

"Over here!" Nathan called.

Moments later a small light came bobbing out of the trees. His heart jumped. She'd found a flashlight. It was a little dim, though, he noted.

"Couldn't find the blue flashlight," she said. "But this one just had a bad connection."

"Looks a little dim," Taylor said dubiously.

"Look," Nathan said, "why don't you guys all

head back while there's still a little light left?
Daley and I will keep following the trail of broken
branches."

"Excellent idea!" Eric said.

"Totally!" Taylor said.

"See ya!" Eric said.

Taylor and Eric were gone within seconds.
Melissa gave Nathan a wincing smile, then
shrugged. "I better check on Jackson," she said.

And then she was gone, too.

"Quitters!" Daley said. "God, I hate quitters."

"Let's just stay positive and keep focused on
finding his trail," Nathan said, "while this battery's
still holding out."

Daley's face was a grim mask as she scanned
the foliage.

"There!" she said. "Another broken branch."

They moved forward into the darkening
jungle.

"Hm-hm hm-hm hm-hmmm-hmmm, ha-
huh ha-huh ha-huhhh-huhhhhh. Hm-hm hm-hm
hm-hmmm-hmmm, ha-huh ha-huh ha-huhhh-
huhhhhh. Hm-hm hm-hm hm-hmmm-hmmm, ha-
huh ha-huh ha-huhhh-huhhhhh."

Lex's humming had grown slower and slower,
softer and softer. But he kept going, putting one
foot in front of the other as he moved up the dark

hillside. He was beginning to lose faith that he'd ever find the ocean. Certainly not tonight, anyway.

And where was the red bird? If the bird had abandoned him—well, he just wasn't sure he could make it.

He paused and considered stopping again. A wave of self-pity ran through him. This was really a bummer. Why couldn't he be home, sitting around the house, messing with his computer?

And then he heard a sound, not far in front of him.

MEEEOOOWWW!

It was the bird, with its goofy cat-sounding call.

He staggered up the hill with renewed strength, jamming his walking stick into the rocky soil. The ridge was only another, what, thirty feet maybe?

"Hm-hm hm-hm hm-hmmm-hmmm, ha-huh ha-huh ha-huhhh-huhhhhh."

And then suddenly, there he was.

The top of the ridge.

He surveyed the horizon. For the first time he was able to see clearly through the trees around him. He was amazed to discover how high he'd climbed.

Up here, unimpeded by branches, the sky seemed much brighter. It was still getting close to dark, several stars visible and the last evidence of the sun only an orange smear on the far horizon.

But that wasn't the best thing. There it was in front of him: *the ocean!*

And best of all . . . it was almost all downhill. As far as he could tell, there was only one more ridge between him and the dark blue rippling surface of the sea!

"Thank yeeewww," said the bird. *"Thank yeewww verrry much!"*

Lex began to run. Suddenly he didn't care about the bag of rocks or the fact that he hadn't had a drink in several hours. He could see the ocean! That was all that counted. He plunged down the long, steep hill, almost falling several times.

But he didn't fall.

And then he headed up the next ridge.

Almost there! he told himself. *Almost there!* Once he reached the beach it would be a simple matter of following the sand all the way back to camp. Even if it took a couple of hours, there would be no problem doing it in the dark. He was totally home free!

His lungs were burning and his muscles aching as he tore up the next ridge. The bag of rocks swung back and forth, but he didn't even notice.

Almost there! Almost there! He stabbed at the ground with his stick, heading up and up. "Hm-hm hm-hm hm-hmmm-hmmm, ha-huh ha-huh ha-huhhh-huhhhhh." Now the humming was coming faster and faster.

Fifty feet. Forty. Thirty.

"Hm-hm hm-hm hm-hmmm-hmmm, ha-huh ha-huh ha-huhhh-huhhhhh."

And then he was there! He reached the crest of the next hill and prepared to leap over, make the final sprint to the sea.

But then—to his horror—he stopped, waving his arms furiously, trying to stop his forward progress.

His heart hammered in his chest.

He was standing on the edge of steep, terrifying cliff. Below him there was no beach. Only a tangle of sharp black rocks, pounded by the waves.

His heart sank. There was no way he'd reach the beach tonight. Too dark, too much chance of slipping and falling on one of these hills, or wandering back into the jungle and getting lost. Two steps forward, or two steps back—either way was dangerous.

What am I gonna do? he thought. Then he looked around for the red bird.

But the bird was gone. He was completely alone.

The flashlight was getting dimmer.

Nathan and Daley had found the last broken branch about fifteen minutes ago. But since then— no success.

"It's got to be here!" Daley said, for about the fifth time.

Nathan was starting to feel doubtful. Up until this point, Lex had broken a branch every twenty feet or so. But now? Nothing.

Suddenly the world went black.

"Nathan!" Daley said. She sounded panicked, on the verge of hysteria.

Nathan thumped the flashlight with the heel of his hand and it flickered back on, revealing Daley, wide-eyed. "No problem," Nathan said. "Melissa said there was something funky in the wiring. We just have to thump it every now and then."

Daley looked around helplessly.

Nathan hated to admit it, but the trail had gone cold. For whatever reason, Lex had stopped breaking branches out here.

"Daley," Nathan said softly, "we need to start heading back."

Daley's jaw was firm. "No."

"We're not going to find him tonight. We've probably got ten or fifteen minutes left in this flashlight, then we're just gonna be sitting here in the dark."

"No." Daley stood rigid as a sentry.

"Daley . . ." Nathan understood how she felt. "Come on. He's probably sleeping out here. We'll get some rest; we'll all get up at first light, and we'll come find him."

He might as well have been talking to a rock. "No," she said again.

"Daley, he's a smart kid. As soon as the sun comes up, he'll get oriented. He'll head for the ocean. He'll be *fine*."

She shook her head, back and forth, back and forth, like once she started, she couldn't stop.

Nathan stepped toward her. "Get away from me," she said.

The light went out again. Nathan had to thump it three times to get it to come back on.

When he looked at her, tears were streaming down Daley's cheeks.

"I should have been with him!" she said. "He's my responsibility!"

"We'll find him in the morning," Nathan said. He was trying to sound as calm and reasonable as possible. Trying to sound more certain than he felt.

Daley didn't move.

He reached out and took her hand. When he turned and began walking back toward camp, she didn't resist.

By the time they reached the shelter, the flashlight had faded to a small yellow button of light about as bright as a firefly.

When they stepped into the shelter, everyone

looked up at them with wordless expectation. They didn't speak, but even in the dark Nathan could read the question in their faces.

He shook his head.

For a long time, no one said anything.

Finally Daley drew herself up and took a deep breath. "How's Jackson?" she said.

There was another silence, then Melissa said, "Something's wrong. I can't get him to wake up."

THIRTEEN

For Daley the night seemed to last a year.
By the time the moon came up, she had thought of just about every bad thing that could possibly happen. Lex had fallen down a crevasse in the rocks where he would die a lingering death of starvation and dehydration. Lex had been attacked by wild pigs and was slowly bleeding to death while she was lying here doing nothing. He had found a volcanic vent, slipped in, and been roasted to death by magma. He had come back to camp unnoticed and then gone swimming and been caught in a riptide and drowned. Or stung by jellyfish, had an allergic reaction, and gone into shock. Or been eaten by a shark. Or attacked by crazed wild monkeys. Or caught whatever Jackson had and was lying in the bushes somewhere, weak with fever.

Once she'd come up with a list of possibilities, they rotated around and around in her head like a bunch of rocks in a clothes dryer.

Then, by midnight, she had everyone in the camp suffering from some kind of terrible tropical disease, all of them slowly succumbing to fever, eventually going blind, losing their voices, hallucinations coming on, and then finally each one in turn slipping into a coma.

She imagined a floatplane landing in the bay, taxiing to the shore, a bunch of rescuers arriving only to find the camp strewn with dead bodies.

She imagined a tall, dark-haired man in a military uniform kneeling over her, lifting her limp arm, then letting it drop to the sand with a soft thump.

We're too late, she imagined the man intoning melodramatically to his copilot. *Twenty-four hours earlier? We could have saved them all . . .*

Daley sat up sharply. "God!" she said softly. "This is ri*dic*ulous."

"You too?" Melissa whispered.

Taylor sat up. "Me too."

Normally the girls slept in the tent and the boys slept in the shelter. But today, in their general state of exhaustion and anxiety, they'd just all collapsed together in the shelter. Eric and Nathan both sat up, too.

"Everything will be better in the morning," Nathan said. "I promise."

Jackson stirred and moaned in his sleep.

"I just feel so helpless," Daley said. "I should have been there for him!"

There was an awkward silence.

"Can I suggest something?" Eric said.

Daley shrugged.

"Look, whatever happens in the morning, happens." He paused. "But right now, how about we talk about something else?"

"How can you say that?" Melissa said. "With Jackson lying right there—"

"Eric's right," Nathan said. "We can sit here in the dark thinking of every worst-case scenario. And we probably all have . . ."

Everybody laughed sheepishly.

"But morning's gonna come a lot sooner," Eric said, "if we think of something else to talk about."

"Like what?" Melissa said.

"Remember what Jackson said?" Eric said. "What would you do if no one was looking?"

There was an uneasy silence.

"Well . . ." Nathan said finally, "everybody has stuff they like to do. But it's just stupid stuff."

"Like what?" Eric's voice had a ring of challenge.

"Uh . . ." Nathan didn't say anything.

"Tell you what," Eric said. "I'll go first. You guys have no respect for me, anyway. I'll tell you what I do if nobody's watching. But everybody else has to agree to tell what they do, too."

"Like truth or dare," Taylor said.

"Just truth," Eric said.

Everybody looked around nervously.

"What have we got to lose?" Eric said. "Nothing!"

"Okay," Melissa said.

Slowly heads began to nod around the circle. Everyone nodded except Daley. Finally everyone was staring at her.

"You first, Eric," she said.

Eric didn't speak for a long time. Finally he cleared his throat. "I volunteer at a home for retarded—I mean, mentally disabled children."

Taylor laughed loudly. "Come on! Be serious!"

Eric's face was barely visible in the moonlight. But he looked totally embarrassed. "I am serious!" he said. Then he scowled. "Man, I don't even know why I suggested this."

"You?" Daley said. "You, the most selfish guy on the planet, *you* volunteer at a home for retarded kids?"

He shrugged, looked at the ground. "My mom used to go there for some women's group she's a member of. It's just around the corner from where I live. She stopped going after a couple of weeks. So I started sneaking out and doing stuff."

"*Why?*" Taylor said.

Eric shook his head. "I don't know. Maybe it's

because they don't care. They don't care if they walk around with their hair sticking up. They don't care if they have jelly on their face. They don't care if they get good jobs or drive a Beemer." He squinted off into the darkness. "Plus, they laugh at my jokes."

"What do you do?"

"I don't know. Whatever. Clean up. Feed kids. Wipe their noses. Play music. Dance. Tell jokes." He shrugged.

Nathan shook his head. "Man, I don't see it."

Eric's eyes narrowed slightly. "What about you?"

Nathan cleared his throat. "I pass."

"You can't *pass*!" Eric said.

"I'll tell you. But not yet. In a minute."

Eric glared at him. "You're a wuss."

"Hold on, hold on," Melissa said. "I'll tell you about me."

"Good idea," Nathan said.

"I like to cook," she said.

"So . . ." Eric said. "That's not embarrassing. You're a girl."

"Hey!" Daley said.

"Yeah, see, but here's the thing," Melissa said. "My family has known what I was going to do with my life since before I was born."

"What do you mean?"

"My mom's a doctor. My dad's a doctor. They've just assumed I was going to be a doctor all my life. They talk about what specialty I should go into. What pays the best, what gets the most respect among other doctors, where I should practice, where I should go to medical school, what I should major in . . ."

"That kinda blows," Eric said.

"I just like to cook," Melissa said. "I mean, I work hard in school and everything. But really, I'd like to be a chef."

"You ever told this to your parents?" Daley said.

Melissa's eyes widened. "Are you *joking*? They'd kill me!"

"Daley?" Nathan said.

"You first."

"No, you first."

"No, you first."

"Oh, puh-lease!" Taylor said. "You're both wimps."

Daley and Nathan turned toward her. "Then what do you like to do?"

Taylor batted her eyes. "Me?"

"Yeah, you!" Nathan said. "And don't tell us you like to do your nails, because we already know that."

Taylor wrinkled her nose. "After we get back?" she said. "If anybody breathes a word of this, you are totally dead meat!"

"This is gonna be good," Eric said, rubbing his hands together.

"Seriously!" Taylor said. "Everybody has to totally swear they'll never tell anyone. Ever."

"Okay, whatever," Nathan said.

The group waited expectantly.

Finally Taylor said, "I play the cello."

There was a brief silence. "You what?" Eric said.

"The cello. I play the freakin' cello. There. Now, I said it!"

Eric said, "You mean like . . ."

"Yeah, like string quartet, classical music, the whole bit. I play the freakin' stupid cello!" Taylor seemed almost comically angry. "And, just so you know? I totally dig it!"

Nathan started laughing. "What's the big deal?"

"The big deal?" Taylor gawked at him. "I'm Taylor Hagan. I am the most popular, coolest, prettiest, most stylish girl at the coolest high school in Los Angeles. I'm not bragging—hey, it's just a fact! Playing cello? That's like the most total geek loser thing in the world."

"All the time we went out and you never told me this?" Nathan felt a peevish note creep into his voice.

"Duh!" Taylor said. "What do you think I was doing when I said I was going to the tanning salon?"

"I kinda figured . . . *tanning*?" Nathan said.

Taylor rolled her eyes. "Nobody tans anymore.

That was like the seventies or something."

"So are you actually, like . . . good?" Eric said.

"Of course I'm good!" Taylor said. "I'm first chair cellist for the LA County Youth Symphony."

"You're not shamming?" Eric said. "You really can play, like . . . Beethoven and Bach and all that stuff?"

"I love the cello! I totally *love* it!" She put her hands over her face. "God, it's so sickening!"

Suddenly the whole group dissolved into laughter. Taylor glared around the circle. Pretty soon every single kid in the group was doubled over laughing. And then Taylor was laughing, too.

It took about five minutes for the laughter to subside. When everybody had finally stopped laughing there was another lull in the conversation. Then everybody turned to Nathan and Daley.

"Okay, guys," Eric said.

"He's first," Daley said

"No way!"

"Way!"

"Forget it! You're first."

"No, you."

"No, *you*!"

"No—"

"HEY!"

Suddenly everyone went silent. All heads turned toward the lump lying on the edge of the platform. The voice they'd just heard was Jackson's.

"I'm trying to get some sleep here," he

whispered. His yell seemed to have taken all his strength.

"Sorry," everybody whispered.

Then they kept looking at him.

"Oh, for Pete's sake," Jackson said. "Daley reads romances and Nathan's a member of the Society for Colossal Anachronism."

Nathan felt a flush rise to his cheeks. His big secret was out! He turned to Jackson. "But how did you—"

"I keep my eyes open," Jackson said. "Instead of thinking about myself all the time, I watch other people."

"Hold on, hold on, hold on, dude," Eric said. "The Society for Colossal Anachronism? Isn't that the group where everybody pretends to be knights in armor and they fight with wooden swords and they have names like Sir Thunderpants and they walk around at Renaissance festivals wearing tights and hanging root-beer mugs off their belts and—"

"It's not a mug!" Nathan said defensively. "It's called a *flagon*."

Everybody started laughing like crazy.

"Yeah, yeah, hilarious," Nathan said.

"What about tights?" Taylor said. "Is it true you wear tights?"

"No!"

Eric looked at him skeptically. "Nathan. Truth, dude. Truth."

"Well . . ." Nathan cleared his throat. "It just so happens that the historically authentic . . ." His voice dropped away to nothing.

"What you're saying is you *do* wear tights," Daley said.

Nathan felt his face heat up again as everybody dissolved into laughter. Daley, in particular, seemed to think this was extremely amusing.

"Hey!" Nathan's voice rose. "Let's hear about your obsession with trashy romance novels, Daley!"

"It's not an obsession! I just happen to like reading . . ." She stopped.

"Yeah, let's hear it," Melissa said.

Daley had a self-conscious smile on her face. "Okay, yeah, they're totally dumb. I admit, guilty as charged. I read the dumbest, trashiest romance novels. So there. Now you know. Hope you're all happy."

After everybody stopped laughing, Nathan said, "Okay, Jackson. You've been lying there listening to everybody else. What's your deep, dark secret?"

Jackson didn't reply.

"Come on, Jackson," Daley said. "Fair's fair."

A tiny grin appeared on Jackson's face. "Not in a million years," he said.

Everybody bombarded him, trying to get him to tell them what his secret was.

When everybody finally got quiet, Jackson

said, "Oh. One other thing. Eric's lying. He wouldn't wipe a retarded kid's nose if you paid him."

Everybody turned toward Eric. He blinked innocently.

"Oops," Eric said.

"You jerk!" Taylor started hitting him.

"Ow! Ow! Ow!" Eric retreated to the other side of the shelter, trying to get away from the furious onslaught.

When the laughter finally stopped, the shelter was quiet.

"So," Nathan said. "What does any of this have to do with starting a fire?"

No one spoke.

"I mean, that was what Jackson said, right? We're supposed to use our embarrassing little obsessions to help us make fire."

"I guess . . ." Melissa said dubiously.

"No, he's right!" Eric said. "Why didn't we think of it? We'll start a fire first thing tomorrow. With . . ."

"With what?" Nathan said.

"With a pair of your tights!"

"Jerk," Nathan said.

Nathan lay back, put his arms behind his head, and stared at the ceiling. And for some reason, he began to smile.

FOURTEEN

The next morning Daley was up as soon as the light began to creep into the sky.

"Okay, guys," she said, clapping her hands. "Everybody up!"

Eric groaned and covered his head with his pillow. "I'm sleeping," he muttered.

Daley yanked the pillow viciously out of his hands. His head bounced on the floor.

"Ow! Hey!" he said.

"Lex is still out there in the woods somewhere," Daley said, clapping her hands again. "Let's go, let's go!"

While Daley was getting everyone organized to hunt for Lex, Melissa checked on Jackson. Once again she couldn't seem to rouse him. His eyes opened and he stared at her. But he didn't speak. She managed to get a few ounces of water into him, but most of it seemed to dribble down his shirt and into his sleeping bag.

She put his head down gently and let him drift off again.

Then she ran out to see if the jungle-medicine book had dried off anymore. She was happy to see that the pages she'd opened to the previous night were fluttering in the early-morning breeze.

Yes! It was starting to dry out. She imagined that no one in history had been so happy to see the word *vomit* at the top of a page.

She carefully read through the information.

"You ready to go?" Daley said.

"I'm reading about vomiting."

Daley looked impatient. "Lex is out there in the woods," she said.

"Yeah, and if we don't figure out what's wrong with Jackson . . ."

Daley sighed. "I know, I know." She bent over and looked at the book. "What have you found out?"

"Well, we already decided that he was the only one who'd drank unboiled water, right?" Melissa said.

Daley nodded. Melissa carefully turned the pages. They had dried overnight—but they were still stuck together. She had to work slowly and carefully to keep them from tearing.

"Okay, here we go . . ." she said.

Nathan walked over and bent over her other

shoulder. "Right there. 'Giardia: an infection of the gut caused by a waterborne protozoan.'"

"Eeyew!" Taylor said.

Nathan kept reading. "'Giardia is usually caused by drinking contaminated water.'"

"Why did he think we were boiling all that water?" Daley said. "Because we like drinking hot water?"

"It was a mistake," Melissa said. "He thought the water in the cooler had been boiled. But it hadn't."

Nathan ran his finger down the page. "'Giardia results in severe diarrhea and vomiting.'"

"Will it just go away?" Taylor said.

"I'm reading about that," Nathan said. "Let's see . . . 'Symptoms may abate. If untreated, certain strains, however, will cause dehydration and electrolyte imbalances with consequences which can be—'"

"Okay, let's not go there," Daley said.

"Is there any way to treat it?" Melissa said. "I mean, the first-aid kit we've got has a whole bunch of stuff in it."

Nathan scanned the rest of the page. "Okay. 'Treatment. Giardia can be effectively treated by application of a broad-spectrum antibiotic such as—'"

"Hey!" Melissa said, feeling her general sense of gloom lift for the first time since Jackson got sick. "There's a bottle of some kind of antibiotic pills in the first-aid kit, isn't there?" she said excitedly.

"Yeah," Daley said. "You guys give him his first dose, and I'll go out to where the trail ends. You can meet me out there."

"I'll come with you," Nathan said.

Daley smiled at him gratefully. "Thanks."

Melissa quickly ran to the girls' tent, where the first-aid kit was stored. She popped the top to the large plastic case and looked inside. Just seeing all the medical equipment made her feel better. Forceps, gauze, Band-Aids . . .

She rifled quickly through the kit. She remembered seeing the antibiotics. They'd been in a brown plastic pill bottle with a white top. Aspirin, bandage scissors, hemorrhoid cream—okay, gross!

But where were the antibiotics?

She searched again, desperately—eventually taking out every single item in the kit, one by one, and setting them on the floor of the tent.

The antibiotics were gone!

FIFTEEN

When Lex woke up, it took him a minute to figure out where he was.

Then he remembered: *Oh, yeah, I'm on top of a cliff.*

He stood up and found himself on a stretch of white rock, five feet from the edge of the cliff. He noticed that the entire right side of his body was white. *Good thing I didn't roll over much in my sleep!* he thought. He sat up and ran his finger across the rock. It was soft and chalky. In fact, he realized, that's probably exactly what it was: chalk. Natural chalk.

When the island had formed, it must have pushed up some of the ocean bottom where chalk had formed a zillion years ago. *Cool!* he thought.

Lex stretched. His legs were sore and his feet

were killing him. And his mouth felt like a bag of sand. He needed some water big-time!

But still he didn't feel bad at all. In fact, he felt great.

He looked around. What an amazing view! From where he was standing, he could see 360 degrees around himself. All the way to the mountain. All the way to the blindingly white horizon. Down to his right he could see the plane wreck on the beach. It wasn't even that far away. Maybe a mile or two?

He smiled. Last night he had felt like he was a million miles from home. During the night he had felt more scared and alone than he'd ever felt in his life. But now it was like a bad dream.

He just wished he had some water.

But, hey—a short little hike and he'd have water to burn. All he had to do was skirt around the marsh and the little inlet where Daley had fallen in and he'd be home free. He picked up his bag of rocks and started to go down the hill.

Which was when he noticed a thin black stripe in the chalky white ground. Then another. Then another. It almost made the top of the cliff look like a giant zebra. Huh. It was kind of a cool-looking rock. He whacked at the rock with his walking stick. A piece chipped off and rolled a few feet down the hill.

Lex leaned over to pick it up, then held it up to the early-morning sun. The black rock had fractured cleanly, almost like glass. But it wasn't obsidian. He'd found some of that already. When you cracked it off this thinly, you could practically see through obsidian. This was different—duller and not quite so transparent. Plus, this stuff had muted bands of color in it.

His eyes widened. Flint! This was a piece of flint!

He whooped loudly and punched the air with his fist.

"Flint, baby!" he yelled. "I found flint!"

Then something struck him. All this time, he'd been thinking of flint as an igneous rock, something spewed out by a volcano. But it wasn't. It was sedimentary. He'd been looking in the wrong place the whole time. What a dope! He laughed. The funny thing was, if he'd thought about it for a few minutes, he'd have remembered that flint had bands of color in it. Bands of color like that were usually found in sedimentary rock, because sedimentary rocks were formed when dirt and stuff got squashed together under a lot of pressure over millions of years.

And since the island was volcanic, he would have assumed there were no sedimentary rocks at all. In which case he'd never have gone out here in the first place, never have gotten lost . . . and never found the flint.

Was there some kind of lesson in that?

Not sure.

He chipped off several more pieces of flint with a fist-size rock from his pack. The flint didn't spark or anything. But theoretically it should when struck on a piece of steel. Well, he'd get that all worked out when he got back to camp.

After he'd knocked off a handful of flint, he hoisted his pack.

"Time for water!" he said.

Then he started down the hill, heading toward camp. As he walked, he looked around, hoping to see the red bird.

Then he thought about it a little more. Had there really even *been* a red bird? A red bird that did an Elvis imitation?

The whole thing seemed a little crazy. He decided he'd skip that part of the story when he got back to camp.

SIXTEEN

"**L**ex! Lex!"

Daley and Nathan called loudly as they hurried along the trail, following the line of broken branches. Daley felt an agonizing clutching sensation in her chest.

"Lex!" Nathan called.

But there was still no answer.

"How could I have done this?" Daley said. "I just let him walk out into the middle of some wild jungle. He's ten years old! What's wrong with me?"

"You didn't do anything wrong," Nathan said.

"Yes I did!" Daley said angrily.

"Okay, okay, fine," Nathan said, somewhat testily. "You're a bad sister and an irresponsible person."

They reached the spot where they had stopped

searching the night before.

"Lex!" Daley shouted. "Lex!" Her throat was sore from screaming for him the night before. But she didn't care. No amount of pain was too much right now—not after letting her brother down like this.

Nathan scanned the area. It was a particularly dark, gloomy area. The ground was covered with a thick layer of rotten leaves so that the jungle seemed to swallow their voices completely.

"Let's look around and see if we missed any broken branches."

They searched for several minutes, but there were no more broken branches. The trail simply ended here.

After a moment Eric and Taylor joined them. Daley took a deep breath. "Let's get ourselves organized," she said. "It's not gonna do us any good to just blunder around."

For once Eric didn't complain about her mania for organization. "Sure," he said. "Whatever you think's best."

Daley briefed the other kids on what she and Nathan had found, how the trail had ended. As she was about to explain her strategy for conducting the search, Melissa burst out from behind a bush, eyes wild.

"Where are the pills?" Melissa shouted frantically.

"What?" Daley said.

"The pills! The antibiotics! They're gone!"

Daley felt mildly irritated at being interrupted. "They're in the first-aid kit," she said.

"No, they're not!"

Daley was feeling intense pressure to get started with the search. She sighed loudly. "Melissa, I inventoried the first-aid kit. The antibiotics were there. Metro . . . metrodizan . . . metronidaz—I forget what they're called."

"They're not!" Melissa's eyes were brimming up with tears. "I took everything in the kit out. They're just not there."

Daley looked around the group. "Did someone take them?"

They all shook their heads.

"I happen to have noticed that a lot of stuff has gone missing," Taylor huffed.

"Like what?" Eric said.

"Well, some of the fishhooks," Taylor said. "And the—"

"Okay, okay!" Daley held up her hands. "Has anyone seen the antibiotics?"

They all shook their heads.

"Does anyone know where they are?"

More head shaking.

Daley spread her hands. "I don't know what to tell you, Melissa. When we get back to camp, we'll find them."

"But . . . Jackson's really in trouble. I gave him

some more water and he couldn't even keep it down. We need to—"

"Melissa! Focus!" Daley felt like she was about to explode. It wasn't that she was mad at Melissa. But they couldn't afford to sit around blabbing about something that they couldn't fix. "It says in the book that you can recover from giardia. But Lex wouldn't have just stayed out here if there wasn't something wrong. Every minute counts!"

"What," Melissa said hotly. "And every minute doesn't count with Jackson?"

Usually Melissa could be counted on to back down if anybody pushed her. But apparently Jackson had some kind of weird effect on her. Daley pointed her finger at Melissa. "Now hold on a minute—"

"Tell you what," Nathan said, stepping in between the two girls. "How about this: We haven't had breakfast. We've got to eat sometime, right? We'll search for an hour. Hopefully that's all it'll take to find Lex. If we don't find him in an hour, we'll take a break, we'll go back, we'll tear the camp apart. The antibiotics didn't get up on their legs and walk away. So we'll find them. Okay?"

Melissa was still glaring at Daley. Daley felt a little bit bad for trying to push her around. But only a little bit. Lex's life was more important than being all sweet and nice to everybody.

"Okay?" Nathan repeated. "An hour."

"*Two* hours," Daley said.

"Okay," Melissa said. "Two. But that's it."

"Okay. So let's not waste any time," Daley said. "Here's what we're gonna do. This point where we're standing is the last place where we know he was. The trail dies here. So we'll go out in a line and we'll circle. Taylor, you'll stay close to the circle, then Melissa, then Nathan, then Eric, then me. Keep in visual contact with whoever is on both sides of you. We'll just make a great big circle."

Daley felt better now that they had a plan.

"If you see anything that looks like a trail," Nathan added, "just call out."

"Like, what's a trail look like?" Taylor said.

"Anything," Nathan said. "A piece of his clothing, another broken branch, footprints, an empty water bottle. Anything."

"Blood?" Eric said.

Daley felt something twist inside her.

"Even that," Daley said.

"Well, let's hope it doesn't come to that," Nathan said.

Jackson lay in the sleeping bag, fading in and out of sleep. In the back of his mind, he knew he was in trouble. He'd been seeing weird things. One time he thought he saw some of his old high-school buddies, Samoan guys, from Chavez High.

Another time he thought he heard a car driving around. He could identify the car just from the sound. It was a hopped-up Acura engine with a turbocharger, just like the one he'd been working on a couple of weeks ago. He could hear it revving up and then—*SCREEEEEE!!!*—the turbo kicking in.

At the same time, he knew it wasn't real. There were no roads on the island, no cars, no turbocharged engines.

It was the oddest thing! He knew he was losing it. And yet he was so exhausted that it didn't even seem to matter.

Part of his mind was still clear. The part that said he was using up all his electrolytes. The part that said he was dehydrated. The part that said he was hallucinating. The part that said this was the stage that came before . . . well . . . the final stage.

He propped himself up on his elbow. Melissa had left him a bottle of water. He took a long pull, then lay back down. The water felt nice, sliding around in his parched mouth. Maybe it would actually stay down this time.

He lay for a couple of minutes. Then suddenly a spasm ripped through his stomach.

Oh, no! he thought. *Not again!*

Then he heard voices again, voices singing. *What a dumb cliché,* he thought distantly. *Sounds like a choir of angels.*

A horrible scream cut through the air.

Daley's heart suddenly jumped into her throat. It was Taylor. She began sprinting through the trees toward the sound.

"Oh God!" Taylor screamed. "Oh, God!"

Nathan and Daley burst out next to Taylor at exactly the same time. "What is it?" shouted Daley.

"What's wrong?" Nathan said.

Taylor pointed mutely. Daley turned to see what she was pointing at. Was Lex lying there dead under a bush or something? Her mind immediately conjured up all the most terrible possibilities—her brother lying there covered in blood . . .

"What!" Daley said. "Where?"

Taylor clutched onto Nathan, still pointing. Her hand shook. "It's so horrible!" she whispered.

Suddenly Nathan's shoulders sagged. "No . . ." he said.

"What?" Daley could barely speak. She had never been so frightened in her life. Not even when the plane had crash-landed on the island.

"No," Nathan said again. "Tell me you're not screaming because of that spider."

Then Daley saw it, a huge hairy spider about the size of the palm of her hand. It sat in the middle of a large web about ten feet away, swaying gently in the breeze. "It's so . . . disgusting! God, I hate spiders!" Taylor squealed.

Daley felt her face harden. "Maybe you should have thought of that before you decided to go camping in the tropics," she said.

Taylor was still clutching Nathan's shoulders. "Okay, Taylor," Nathan said, pushing her away. "I think you lost grabbing-hold-of-Nathan privileges when you ditched me on the last day of school."

"Yeah, but—"

"Taylor," Daley said, "if you scream like that again for no good reason, I will personally . . . I will personally . . ." She was so mad, she couldn't even think of what she would do. The way Taylor had screamed, she had thought for sure that Lex was dead. "Well, you'll be sorry, that's all I have to say."

She waved her hands. "False alarm. Everybody back to the search."

They had been searching for an hour and forty-five minutes, continually widening the circle. But so far, no sign of Lex. As the deadline for the breakfast break grew closer, Daley got more and more queasy.

She drove the other kids as hard as she could, pushing them to search more diligently, to move faster, to be more thorough. And, to their credit, nobody grumbled—not even Eric. Daley was almost looking for someone to blow up at, just so that she could stop thinking about her own failures. But everybody was working hard and doing their best.

She kept trudging through the forest, looking behind bushes, under logs, behind tree trunks. But there wasn't a sign of Lex anywhere. Finally she called out: "Okay, everybody!"

The other kids slowly filtered out of the trees and gathered around her. The were all dirty, sweaty, and tired-looking. Even Taylor had bits of bark in her hair, dirt under her fingernails, a smudge on her cheek.

"Look," Daley said, a note of pleading creeping into her voice. "I know we said we'd take a break for breakfast after two hours. But you think we could do an extra half hour?"

The others looked at her expressionlessly.

Finally Melissa said, "I know how you feel about Lex—"

"No, you don't!" Daley said.

Melissa winced. "Okay, maybe I shouldn't have said it that way. I know you feel responsible for Lex. But we've got *two* people whose lives are in jeopardy right now. If we don't find that medicine for Jackson . . ." She didn't finish her sentence.

"Please!" Daley said. "Fifteen minutes!"

Again, there was silence.

Finally Eric held up his water bottle and turned it upside down. "I'm out of water," he said.

"What if we're looking in the wrong place?" Taylor said.

Daley stamped her foot. "He's ten years old!" she shouted.

Nathan voice was soft as he said, "We know that, Daley. And we'll keep looking. But we need water, we need food, and we need to find those pills."

Daley felt her eyes brimming up with tears of anger and shame and defeat.

Then she noticed something: Eric was pointing, his eyes widening.

"What?" she said.

"Is that . . ." He didn't finish the sentence.

But she saw what he was pointing at. They had reached a slightly hillier section of the island now. And there, on the side of a small hillside rising up next to them, were several red splotches.

They looked like . . .

"Blood!" Taylor said. "Is that blood?"

"You guys stay here," Nathan said.

The splotches were on a somewhat inaccessible ridge above the group. If it was blood, it was definitely fresh. The red was bright and easily visible, not like dried blood. Daley didn't know whether it made her feel good or not. She didn't want Lex to be hurt. But if this meant they were closer to finding him . . .

Daley's heart started beating hard and she heard a roaring in her ears. "I'll go," she said.

But Nathan was already scaling the side of the hill, grabbing hold of bushes and yanking himself upward. She watched helplessly. *Be careful,* she thought. *Don't fall.*

Finally Nathan reached the largest of the red splotches. He stopped and stared down at it.

"What?" Daley said. "What is it?"

He reached over and picked something up, held it in the air. She could just make out what it was. A large red feather.

Melissa gave Daley a brief hug. "We're gonna find him," she said.

Then she turned and began heading back toward camp.

Jackson lay in his sleeping bag, dreaming.

His dreams were strange and disconnected, one thing twisting quickly into another. He dreamed about school, about his mother, about cars, about samurai warriors chasing him around—about all kinds of things. But behind it all there was music.

Not that choirs-of-angels junk he'd been imagining earlier. No, this was something different. This was—

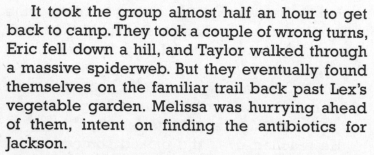

It took the group almost half an hour to get back to camp. They took a couple of wrong turns, Eric fell down a hill, and Taylor walked through a massive spiderweb. But they eventually found themselves on the familiar trail back past Lex's vegetable garden. Melissa was hurrying ahead of them, intent on finding the antibiotics for Jackson.

As they approached the girls' tent, Melissa suddenly held up her hand. She turned and looked curiously at everybody.

"What?" Daley said.

Wordlessly, Melissa held one finger up to her lips.

Daley cocked her head, trying to hear.

Melissa motioned for them to join her. Daley trotted toward her, stopped, and listened again. She heard waves crashing on the beach. And then, above it, something else—a higher, thinner sound.

"It sounds like somebody singing," Melissa said.

"Yeah, Nathan said. "Sounds like somebody singing—"

Daley broke into a run. She heard it, too. She pounded up the path and crested the small dune near the wreckage.

There, standing in the middle of the beach, was a small figure. The tiny person was silhouetted against the sunlit sea.

And he was dancing. Dancing like crazy, shaking his hips, holding something that looked like a microphone up to his lips.

"Well, since my baby left me!" he howled. Then he did double bump with his hips. "I've found a new place to dwell!"

"Elvis!" Nathan said.

"Elvis!" Jackson said, sitting up. And there it was.

His dream was gone, but he could still hear the singing.

"Elvis!" Taylor said. "Lex is singing Elvis!"

There was a brief moment of shock. Then everyone—except Daley—dissolved into nearly hysterical laughter.

Lex must have heard them, because he suddenly stopped dancing and singing. Then he whirled around and stared at them. The piece of wood he'd been holding in his hand like a microphone fell to the sand.

"Uh . . ." he said.

Daley raced toward him.

Then she grabbed him and swept him up in her arms.

"Oh, hi," Lex said.

Daley kept squeezing him and squeezing him. "Okay, okay," Lex grunted. "Glad to see you, too. But you're kinda squashing me."

Daley let go of him and pushed him away so she could look at him. "Where have you been?" she said. "I'm gonna kill you!"

"Well, that's a somewhat interesting story," Lex said.

"Elvis," Jackson said. "Coulda sworn I heard someone singing Elvis."

Then he lay back down and fell asleep again.

SEVENTEEN

Everyone was sitting around the fire ring. Everybody but Melissa, that is. While everyone else ate, Melissa began working her way methodically through the camp looking for the antibiotics. She started by slowly taking every single item out of what was left of the plane and tossing it on the sand.

"Well, I have an announcement to make," Lex said proudly. "You'll all be interested to know that—"

"Okay, people!" Taylor interrupted. "We gotta find those pills. Melissa's gonna go postal on us in a minute."

Everyone else watched her as they munched contentedly on dried fruit.

"What pills?" Lex said.

Daley explained that they had figured out

what was wrong with Jackson and that he needed antibiotics.

"Isn't that strange?" Lex said. "I noticed something missing the other day."

"The camp knife?" Nathan said.

"No, something else." Lex couldn't quite remember what it was.

"Speaking of bad water," Nathan said. "Has anybody made any progress on starting a fire? 'Cause I'm still striking out."

"Well, as a matter of fact—" Lex said.

Eric stood up and started walking away from the group.

"Hey," Daley called. "Where are you sneaking off to?"

"Huh?" Eric gave her his usual innocent expression. "Me?"

"If you're done eating, go help Melissa," she commanded.

"*Okay!*" he said. Then he started shuffling over toward the remains of the plane where Melissa was working.

"So as I was saying . . ." Lex said. As usual, whenever he had something to say, nobody listened.

"As you were saying . . ." Nathan curled his lip a little and struck an Elvis pose. "Thank yeew, thank yeww verrry much!"

Everybody laughed.

Lex flushed.

"Look, guys," Daley said. "We could sit here making fun of Lex Presley all morning—in fact, I intend to make fun of him for the rest of his life—"

Again everybody died laughing.

"You people are real comedians," Lex said.

"Anyway," Daley said, "we really should start looking for those antibiotics. Nathan, you look in the area where the boys' tent was when it blew away. Maybe somebody put them in there and they got blown away. Taylor, you check the girls' tent. Open everybody's stuff if you have to. I'll check the shelter."

Everybody stood up.

Lex raised his voice. "Um, actually, before you get started—"

"Oh, I forgot about you," Daley said. "Lex, after what you just went through, I want you to rest and hydrate. Okay? Go straight to bed."

"Daley!" Lex was getting frustrated. "I have something I need to tell everybody."

"Later," Daley said. "This is important."

Lex watched the big kids all stand up and hustle away.

Bed? Yeah, right.

Lex wandered over to the shelter. He was looking for something to use as a striker with the flint. It needed to be steel. A knife would be ideal.

As Nathan had said, the camp knife seemed to have disappeared. And the machete seemed too unwieldy. So Lex finally settled on a small knife that

Daley had brought. It was a shiny dive knife in an orange plastic sheath. Daley had made a big deal about how it was supposed to be this great stainless steel that wouldn't rust in the ocean.

He went into the woods carrying the knife and his bag of rocks. If nobody was going to listen to him, then he'd conduct a few experiments himself. Maybe he'd just start the fire himself with no help from anybody. Maybe they'd finally listen to him, then!

Here's your fire, guys! I did it. Yeah, that's right, the little geek that nobody listens to? He made your fire and saved your bacon. You're welcome! You're welcome very much!

Big kids. Man, sometimes he got so sick of them.

Eric was in a little bit of a bind right now. He knew that he had to make a move. But he just wasn't quite sure how to do it without catching a giant steaming pile of crap from the other kids.

"Hey, Melissa," he said, "I need to take a quick trip to the, uh . . ." He waved in the direction of the latrine.

"Well, hurry up," she said grimly.

"You know it," he said, grinning.

Then he turned and hustled over in the direction of the latrine. But as soon as he got out of sight of the camp, he turned and took a different path, heading out in the direction of Lex's garden.

Next thing he knew, there was Lex, sitting right next to the garden. He had a bunch of rocks spread out all over the ground. Darn it! Why'd he have to pick this exact spot to do one of his dumb little experiments?

"Hey!" Eric said. "How's the world traveler doing?"

"Fine," Lex said. "Check out what I found."

"Yeah, neat, rocks," Eric said. "So, hey, shouldn't you be in bed? I bet you got pretty dehydrated out there."

"Well, actually, I've got something I need to do."

"Right *here*?" Eric said. "Couldn't do it back at camp?"

"What's wrong with here?"

Eric smiled broadly. "Not a thing, pal. Not a thing!" He slapped Lex on the shoulder. "By the way, fabulous Elvis impersonation."

Eric decided he'd better get back to camp. Otherwise the Let's-Harass-the-Snot-Out-of-Eric Police would be in full force. He hurried away, leaving Lex sitting there with an expression on his face like he'd just bitten down on a piece of rotten fish.

Nathan searched the entire area around where the boys' tent had been before the storm trashed it the other night, then traced the path along which it had blown before it snagged in the trees. It was a sandy area with very little vegetation. There wasn't much of anywhere the pill bottle could have hidden. It just wasn't there.

So he found the torn-up tent, unfurled what was left of it, and peered inside. No pill bottle.

Nathan was starting to get worried. Worried and a little angry. There was no good reason for anybody to have taken the antibiotics out of the first-aid kit. The more he thought about it, the more things seemed to have gone missing recently. A bunch of stuff. Even before the lighter had gotten broken, there had been a mess kit that they cooked in that had mysteriously vanished.

Then there'd been a fishing net. Probably some other stuff, too.

It seemed like it was beyond coincidence.

Somebody had to be taking the stuff. But who? There was no reason to think anybody in the camp would take stuff. But who else would do it? Monkeys?

Not likely.

Nathan walked out onto the sand and began searching up and down the beach. It seemed pretty much impossible that the pills would have been dropped out here. But they were running out of places.

Suddenly he stopped and spotted something on the sand. Not the pill bottles, but a stick.

He picked it up and looked at it. It was the short stick that Lex had been using as a microphone when he was doing his goofy Elvis impression. Which, by the way, was totally weird, huh?

Who'd have thought the kid had it in him?

He looked thoughtfully at the short stick and rubbed the end of it with his thumb. He couldn't believe it! Perfect!

Nathan smiled and tucked the stick in his pocket.

Lex glared after Eric. That guy was so *irritating*. Lex sighed. Oh, well. He pretty much just had to resign himself to the fact that all the big kids would be making Elvis jokes for quite a while.

He pulled the knife out of the sheath, picked up the largest piece of flint, and whacked it against the side of the knife. He expected a nice shower of sparks.

Instead? Nothing. Not a single spark.

Hmm, he thought, *maybe I'm hitting at the wrong angle.*

He tried hitting it at a more oblique angle. Still no sparks. He whacked it harder. Again. Again. And again.

He couldn't believe it. He was sure this was

flint. It had to be. It looked exactly like the flint he'd seen in the museum. And like the ones in his dad's Indian arrowhead collection. He frowned. Maybe it was a problem with that particular stone.

He set down the big one and tried a smaller one. That one didn't work, either. No matter how hard or how soft he whacked it. No matter what angle. No matter what part of the blade he struck it against.

He was getting zero sparks.

He set down the rock and began moving methodically through all the different rocks. Nothing!

His growing sense of disappointment started turning to anger.

"Stupid rock," he muttered as he battered away at the knife. He was now making deep scratches in the metal. "Stupid, stupid, stupid rock!"

He reached the last rock. Still nothing. He battered away, finally taking a chip out of the edge of the blade. He was so mad now that he couldn't stand it. Not only was he a total failure, but now Daley was going to kill him because he'd messed up her knife.

"Stupid rock!" he shouted.

He scooped them all up and heaved them into the bushes next to the trees. They rattled and clattered into the foliage.

Oops, he thought. *Maybe that wasn't so smart.*

When Eric got back to the plane, Melissa was standing outside with her hands on her hips. The entire contents of the plane were now lying in the sand. She looked like she was about to cry.

"No luck, huh?" he said.

"Where were you?" she said.

"Obeying the call of nature," he said. "You want me to get more specific?"

"Gross!" It was Taylor, walking out from behind the plane.

"How about you?" Melissa said, ignoring Eric. "Did you find anything, Taylor?"

Taylor shook her head.

"Are you sure?" Melissa said. "Because if you—"

"Excuse me," Taylor said. "But you are not the only girl on this island who cares about Jackson. Just so we're clear on that."

Eric took that as his cue to slip away from the plane. He saw Nathan heading in his direction, so he changed directions and walked briskly up the trail that led to the shelter.

When he reached the shelter, he looked in and found Jackson lying in a heap.

"Jackson?" he said. "How you doing, buddy?"

Jackson didn't even move.

"Jackson? *Jackson?*"

No answer. Eric rubbed his face. Okay, this was not good. This was really not good. He was just going to have to bite the bullet.

He headed back down the trail toward Lex's garden. But when he reached the garden, he moved off the trail and into the woods, hooking around so that he entered the garden from the rear. He didn't see Lex anywhere.

Better safe than sorry, though. He tiptoed slowly out into the garden and crossed through the neatly laid out rows of little green shoots, toward a particular bush.

Okay! Almost there!

He leaned over and pulled back the leaves of a large banana plant.

Lex had recovered five of the six pieces of flint from the bushes where he'd flung them. He figured five was plenty, so he came back out of the bushes.

As he did, he almost stumbled into a huddled figure, bent over underneath a banana tree.

"Eric?" he said.

Eric stood up like someone had hit him with a cattle prod. "Huh! What! Geez, you scared me!"

Lex stared. Not at Eric. But at the ground next to the banana tree.

There on the ground was a small bundle.

Wrapped in clear plastic he could see a mess kit, a fishnet, and the missing camp knife.

And in Eric's hand was a small brown plastic bottle.

"What's going on here?" Lex demanded.

"Nothing!" Eric said.

Lex looked at him for a long time.

"Look, uh, see, what it is," Eric said, words tumbling out of his mouth, "I just thought it was smart to keep this stuff separate in case there was another storm." He smiled weakly. "Don't want all our stuff blowing away at once, right?"

Lex just glared at him.

"It's true!"

Lex shook his head.

Eric sighed. "Okay. Okay. Fine. You've got me. Busted."

Lex couldn't figure it out. "Why? What are you doing, Eric?"

"I can't sleep, all right? I can't stop thinking about how I don't want to spend the rest of my life on this island." He studied Lex's face. "I mean, doesn't it bother you?"

"Well, sure. It bothers everybody."

"It doesn't feel like it. This shelter we built— it's like we're making a fort or something. Like we're settlers, you know? Like we're planning to stay here forever."

"That shelter is for protection."

"Yeah, well, I don't want protection. I want to

go home!" For once it looked like Eric was being honest. This was clearly no act. Eric was genuinely troubled. "You know how I keep from going crazy? I think up ways to escape. Seriously."

"This isn't a prison."

"To you, maybe," Eric said. "You've got your little garden and your little experiments and your little ... rocks. You've got Daley. Me? I've got nothing. I think I might take off and explore the west side of the island."

"Are you serious? Why didn't you tell anyone?"

"What for? Nobody'd go with me. And if I wanted to take some gear, Daley'd call for another dumb vote and everybody would gang up on me and stop me. That's why I took this stuff. In case I went. I know it's wrong ... but I didn't know what else to do."

"Are you really gonna go?"

Eric shrugged. "I don't know. But at least thinking about it gives me hope."

Lex nodded. He could kind of see where Eric was coming from. It was bad enough knowing people thought your Elvis impression was dorky. Imagine what it would be like to know that everybody thought you were a jerk. Eric must feel incredibly lonely.

"So look ..." Eric looked Lex in the eyes. "Are you gonna tell anybody?"

"I've got an idea," Lex said.

EIGHTEEN

Everyone had gathered in a dejected circle at the shelter.

"So no one found the antibiotics, huh?" Nathan said.

They all shook their heads.

"All I found were more of these weird notes," Daley said. She pulled out a pink note, just like the one she had found the day before. "This one says, 'Better get ready for it!' "

Melissa was sitting next to Jackson, who was sleeping.

"What about you, Mel?" Nathan said.

Melissa held up a small pink piece of paper.

"What does it say?" Nathan said.

"Does it really matter?" Melissa said.

Before anybody had a chance to answer, Lex appeared and jumped up into the shelter.

"I thought I told you to rest," Daley said.

Lex said, "Well, it seemed like this might be slightly more important."

"What might?" Daley said.

Lex reached into his pocket and pulled out a small brown pill bottle.

Melissa's eyes widened. Then she jumped up, grabbed the bottle of antibiotics, and hugged Lex. "Oh, thank you!" she said. "Thank you, thank you, thank you!"

"Where'd you find it?" Daley said.

Lex cleared his throat. "Uh . . . it sort of got into my backpack somehow."

"How did *that* happen?" Daley said.

"Um . . ." Lex said, glancing at Eric for a moment. Nathan wondered what that was about. But he didn't have time to think about it. Melissa was suddenly a whirlwind of action.

"Somebody get some water," Melissa said. Then she shook Jackson. "Wake up! Wake up!"

Jackson looked up groggily, blinking at her.

Daley handed Melissa a bottle of water. "I just hope he can keep it down!" she said as she gave Jackson one of the antibiotic pills, following it up with some water.

Jackson spluttered, swallowed the water, then lay back down and closed his eyes.

"Everybody cross your fingers," Melissa said.

The entire group sat without speaking for

at least ten minutes, watching Jackson as he lay sleeping.

Suddenly Melissa grinned and stood up. "If he hasn't thrown it up yet, I think it'll stay down."

"He's gonna be okay!" Nathan said.

Melissa took a deep breath, then looked around at the group. "Sorry I got so crazy, everybody. It's just . . . I was kinda freaking out."

"Hey, don't even think about it," Nathan said, putting his arm around her shoulder.

After a moment, Melissa turned to Taylor and held up the piece of pink paper. It was crushed from being wadded up in her palm and mottled with water that had spilled while she was giving the pills to Jackson. "Okay, Taylor," she said. "Give it up. What's this all about?"

Taylor smiled mysteriously. "We're a little low on food," she said. "I think I'll go harvest some fruit for us."

Then she sashayed away.

"There's a first," Eric said.

Taylor looked over her shoulder. "Meeting at lunch," she shouted. "All will be revealed!"

NINETEEN

At lunchtime Taylor appeared at the shelter with a basket of fruit in her hands. She placed it ceremoniously in the middle of the group. The fruit was all artfully arranged, like a centerpiece at a restaurant.

"Okay, everybody," she said. "Dig in!"

Nathan looked at Daley.

"I think Taylor's body has been taken over by an alien," Daley said.

"Ha-ha," Taylor said.

"All right, Taylor," Jackson said, sitting up on one elbow. "What's the big secret?"

Taylor's eyes widened. "Look at you! How are you feeling?"

"I've been better," he said. "How about handing me a piece of that fruit?"

Taylor gave him a mango. He wolfed it down.

Everybody applauded.

"What?" he said.

"We're just glad you're back," Daley said.

"But enough about me," Jackson said. "Taylor, you keep dodging the issue. What's the secret?"

Taylor stood up and looked around the group. "Question," she said. "What's the worst part about being stuck on this island?"

"Bad food," Nathan said.

"Sunburn," Daley said.

"No TV," Eric said.

"Sand flies," Lex said.

"After my last two days?" Jackson said. "No toilet paper."

This brought a round of laughter.

"No deodorant," Melissa said.

Everybody turned and looked at Melissa. She shrugged.

"Okay, I change my vote," Eric said. "No deodorant."

The whole group dissolved into laughter. The relief in seeing Jackson's dramatic improvement had brightened everybody's mood.

"All true," Taylor said. "All icky. But I'm talking about something much worse." She paused dramatically. "I'm talking about . . . the smoosh."

"The what?" Melissa said.

"The smoosh!" Taylor spread her arms. "Every day feels the same. How many days have we been here? Thirty? Forty?"

Everybody looked at one another. Nathan frowned. Boy, he couldn't remember. That was strange.

"Seventeen," Lex said.

"Exactly!" Taylor pointed at Lex. "I've lost track of everything. It all smooshes together. I don't even know what day of the week it is."

"Tuesday," Lex said.

"No, it's Wednesday," Daley said.

"I'm pretty sure it's Tuesday," Eric said.

Nathan didn't say anything. He was sort of thinking it was Friday.

"See!" Taylor said. "It's all . . . smooshed! There's nothing to look forward to. Nothing to get excited about. Even weekends don't count because they don't feel any different."

"So I'm still not with you," Daley said. "What's the exciting thing that's coming? A calendar?"

"No! Tomorrow we're going to have something special. Something we haven't had in a long time."

"Ice cream?" Daley said.

"Pizza?" Jackson said.

"Soap," Nathan said.

"Deodorant?" Eric said.

"No!" Taylor grinned broadly and held up her hands like she had just won the Olympics or something. "We're going to have . . . *a holiday!*"

Nathan felt a little confused. He looked around the circle and got the impression he wasn't the only one. Everybody looked puzzled.

"C'mon," Taylor shouted. "Everybody loves holidays!"

"Taylor," Daley said, "can I just point out that tomorrow isn't a holiday?"

"But it is! I made one up."

Everybody chuckled. They were starting to get it.

"You invented a holiday?" Nathan said.

"Yes!" Taylor hadn't looked this excited about anything since they'd landed on the island. "And since I thought of it, I make the rules." She pulled out a notebook—it was the same pink paper that had been used to make all the notes—and began to read. "First, there will be no work because it's wrong to work on a holiday."

"Sounds good," Nathan said. "What else?"

"Second, what kind of holiday would it be without presents? We each have to make a gift for the group."

There was a rumble of disapproval. Nathan was thinking about the fact that they still didn't have a fire, and that the search for Lex and for the pills had eaten up time they normally would have used for gathering food. So they had a lot of work ahead of them just to get their stock of food back to normal. But on the other hand . . .

"Oh, stop whining!" Taylor put her hands on her hips. "It doesn't have to be big."

"I'm not liking this already," Eric said.

"Seriously," Daley said. "This is dumb. We're

totally running behind on all our chores after all the—"

Taylor interrupted her. "Finally, the day will end with a traditional feast. We'll get dressed up and eat and most importantly ... have *fun*!"

Even though there were some problems with the idea, Nathan realized that Taylor was right. Every day they'd been here had been like boot camp—one chore after another. Maybe it *was* time for a break.

"I think it's a great idea," Nathan said.

"Me too!" Melissa chimed in. She'd pretty much been giddy ever since Jackson had started showing signs of improvement.

"Does this holiday have a name?" Jackson said.

"It does," Taylor said. "We worked really hard to save some of the plane, to make the shelter, to find Lex, to ... well, the point is, we've been working hard all week."

"*Some* of us have," Daley said, giving Jackson a poke with her toe.

"Very funny," Jackson said.

"Anyway, the most important thing," Taylor said, "is that it's a day of rest. We're going to forget our troubles and just ... chill. That's why I call it ... Chilloween!"

Everybody laughed at the goofy name except Daley and Eric.

"Jell-O-who?" Lex said.

"Chill-o-*ween!*" Taylor said.

"That doesn't mean anything," Eric said.

"Sure it does! We're all going to chill!" Taylor said. "And then there's . . . like . . . the ween part because . . . oh, who cares, it's just a name."

"I think it's a perfect name," Nathan said. He was getting into the spirit of it already.

"Me too," Melissa said.

Taylor grinned. "See? Can you feel it? The excitement is building, people. It's Chilloween Eve!"

Everybody looked happy. Everybody except Daley.

"C'mon, Daley," Nathan said.

Daley looked around the group and said, "Can I just point out that we have about half a bottle of water left for each of us? And we have no fire."

Nathan was glad to see that Taylor stood her ground. With a grin, she looked around the group and said, "Okay, then, you know what that means?"

They all shook their heads.

"That means that by tomorrow, one of us has to make a fire. That's all there is to it." She held up one fist and pumped it in the air. "Failure is not an option!"

TWENTY

Daley was walking past the shelter, carrying a load of water—just in case anybody actually got the fire started—when Lex called out to her: "Hey! Happy Chilloween Eve!"

"Give me a break," Daley said. Everybody was going around saying "Happy Chilloween" to one another. It was giving her a headache. Just because they'd dodged a couple of bullets today, that didn't mean everybody could relax!

"C'mon!" Lex said. "Everybody's into it."

"Oh, please," Daley said, setting down the heavy jugs of water. "Taylor's just looking for an excuse to get out of work."

"But it's fun!"

"Yeah, right," Daley said. "If everybody buys that, fine. I don't."

She hoisted the water and began lugging it toward the fire ring. The *useless* fire ring.

Nathan figured he'd better get cracking on the fire. He still had the stick he'd found on the beach in his pocket. Lex's "microphone."

He smiled, thinking back at the look on Lex's face when he'd realized that everybody was behind him. It wasn't just that it amused Nathan, though. Lex had been so totally into it. He'd have never guessed the kid had it in him.

Nathan sat down at the fire ring and gathered all his equipment. The new stick, the bow, the tinder, the wooden base, and the smaller wooden drill holder that held the top of the stick. He took the tinder—it was made from the dried fibers of the outside of a coconut—formed it into a small bird's-nest shape, then set it aside.

Next he trimmed the ends of the new drill stick, and then wrapped the bow around it. Then he set everything up and started sawing away. It took a while, but eventually he got a puff of smoke.

"Yes!" he shouted. "Woo!"

"Not you, too?"

He turned, found Daley looking at him with an irritated look on her face. "Why be a party pooper?" he said. "This Chillyweeny thing'll be fun."

"Chillo*ween*," she said.

"Whatever." He pointed at his fire-starting setup. "Besides, I just got smoke!"

"Really?"

"Watch."

He ran his hand back and forth as fast as he could. After a short period of time his arm started burning. About the time he was sure his arm was going to give out on him, a thin wisp of smoke started trailing out of the gap between the stick and the wooden base.

He lifted up the stick excitedly. There was a thin coating of black dust inside the depression in the wood. But no embers. He sighed. "Well, it's working, anyway. The wood's perfect. I just have to get my technique down."

He began yanking back and forth on the bow again.

"Good luck," Daley said glumly.

Just as some more smoke appeared, the bow snapped in half.

"Shoot!" Nathan said.

"See," Daley said. "Nothing's ever as easy as you want it to be." Then she turned and walked away.

Nathan watched her go. "Happy Chilloween to you, too," he said softly.

Eric took the reflector and whacked on it halfheartedly, trying to beat it back into shape. But it was no use.

He must have gotten lucky the other day. It seemed like the more he beat on the thing, the worse it got.

"Happy Chilloween," Melissa said brightly as she walked by, a fishnet looped over her shoulder. "How's it coming?"

"Oh, couldn't be better," Eric said. "This thing's never gonna work."

"Why not?" Melissa said.

"Look, it got all crinkled up when everybody stepped on it the other day. Now it doesn't reflect properly." He threw it across the sand. The wind caught it and tossed it at Melissa's feet.

She frowned and stared down at it.

"Huh," she said.

"What?" he said.

She kept staring at it. "I was just thinking . . ." She didn't finish her sentence.

"You know what?" Eric said. "Either we're gonna have a fire or we're not. But I'm gonna enjoy Chilloween."

Melissa kept staring quizzically at the reflector.

"Okay," Eric said. "I'm outta here."

Melissa didn't even seem to notice as he walked away.

Lex brought his bag of rocks over to the fire ring, sat down, and spread the rocks out in front of him.

"What've you got there?" Nathan said. He was still messing around with his bow-and-drill fire-starter.

"So the reason I went out yesterday?" Lex said. "I went out and looked for rocks."

Nathan smiled, set the bow down, and rubbed his arm. "I heard a little something about that."

"Yeah, well, everybody's been so distracted by all the stuff that's going on that nobody's listened to my story. I'm pretty sure I found flint."

"Yeah?"

"Problem is, I still can't figure out how to strike sparks with it."

Nathan leaned over and picked up one of the rocks. "Looks like flint to me."

"There must be something I'm doing wrong," Lex said. "Something to do with the technique I'm using, maybe."

"Show me."

Lex took out Daley's dive knife, picked up one of the flints, and struck it on the flat side of the blade. "See? Nothing. I've tried hitting like this. Like this. Like this." He showed all the different approaches he'd taken.

"Let me see it." Nathan reached out his hand.

Lex handed him the knife.

Nathan narrowed his eyes and studied the

dinged-up blade. "Boy, you really tore it up," he said. "Daley's gonna have a fit."

"Tell me about it," Lex said.

Nathan handed the knife back. "Well," he said, "there's your problem."

"What?" Lex said. "The knife?"

Nathan nodded.

"What do you mean?"

"It's stainless steel. The only way to strike a spark with flint is to use fully hardened high-carbon steel."

"What's the difference?"

"Stainless steel has a bunch of chromium in it. For some reason that keeps it from throwing off sparks."

Lex frowned. "Well . . . all knives are stainless steel, aren't they?"

"Not necessarily." Nathan had an odd, rueful smile on his face. "Hardly anybody uses carbon steel anymore. It's kinda like a back-in-the-days-of-yore type deal. Hammer and anvil, that kind of thing." Nathan kept smiling.

"What?" Lex said.

"Just so happens," Nathan said, reaching down to his belt and pulling his knife out of his sheath, "I bought this one from a custom knife-maker . . . at a Renaissance festival. I watched him hammer it out on the anvil and everything."

"So how'd you know all this stuff about steel?" Lex said.

Nathan blushed. "What can I say? I've spent way too much time reading about medieval swords." He held the knife out toward Lex. Lex had never even seen it before. It was a small sheath knife with a picture of a knight in armor carved into what appeared to be an ivory handle. "Here."

"Whoa . . . cool!" Lex said, taking the knife.

Nathan laughed. "You're probably the only person here who'd think so."

Lex hefted the knife. It was light and well balanced. The surface of the steel gleamed with oil. Lex felt the edge with his thumb. It was like a razor.

"Go ahead," Nathan said.

Lex blinked. "But . . . it's so beautiful. I'll ruin it."

Nathan shrugged. "It's not the *Mona Lisa*. It's a tool. We need fire."

Lex shook his head. "I can't."

"Go ahead," Nathan said again.

Lex still felt weird about it. Before striking the flint on the knife, there was something else he wanted to talk about. "So let me ask you a question," Lex said. "When you were out there in the jungle looking for me . . . did you see a red bird? A big red bird?"

Nathan shook his head. "Found a couple of big red feathers, though. Why?"

"Well . . ." Lex frowned. "Something weird happened out there."

"What was that?"

"This bird . . ."

"What?"

Lex was sure Nathan would think he was crazy. "This bird did an Elvis imitation."

"It *what*?"

"Yeah. It followed me around. I fed it scraps of coconut and it kept going, 'Thank yew! Thank yew verrry much!' "

Nathan scratched his head. "You're not making this up?"

Lex shook his head. "It was a parrot, I think."

"That's bizarre." Nathan's frowned. "Maybe it was imitating you."

"No. I was singing 'Heartbreak Hotel'. But I don't think I ever did that thank-you-very-much thing."

Suddenly Nathan's eyes widened. "You know what? The pilot of the plane, Captain Russell, he was a big Elvis fan."

"Okay . . ." Lex said.

"I heard him say that three or four times when we first got on the plane. 'Thank you, thank you very much.' " He looked thoughtful. "That bird must have run into Captain Russell and the other kids. They must have fed it. And it heard Captain Russell doing his little Elvis thing."

"Really! So that must mean . . ."

"They're still out there!"

Lex held both hands out wordlessly toward

Nathan, the piece of flint in one hand, the beautiful knife in the other. "Here," Lex said. "You do it. I'd rather not mess up your knife."

But Nathan ignored Lex. He grabbed his bow and drill, then stood up. "I should probably tell Daley about your bird." Nathan turned and disappeared down the trail.

After he was gone, Lex looked down at the flint and the knife in his hands. For a moment he hesitated. But then he thought, *Why would he have given it to me if he didn't want me to use it?*

And with that, he smacked the spine of the knife with the small rock in his hand.

"Oh my God!" Lex said.

And then he felt himself grinning from ear to ear.

TWENTY-ONE

Taylor felt happier than she'd felt in a long time. Fire or no fire, they were going to have fun. She was full of energy.

The first thing she wanted to do was decorate the shelter. There was kind of a shortage of party supplies here, so she was just going to have to improvise. She decided to hang the big orange parachute from the side of the shelter.

As she was struggling to hang the parachute from the logs supporting the thatched shelter, Jackson appeared, walking down the trail from out of the jungle.

"Well, look at you!" she said. "Up and around!"

"Sorta," he said, looking up at her with a bemused expression on his face. "Need help?"

"Well—shouldn't you be resting?"

"I'll be okay for a few minutes," he said. "I'm feeling a lot better."

"Okay. Grab the other end."

He stood on the platform and hooked the edge of the parachute on a piece of wood projecting from the log.

"Higher!" Taylor said. "Spread it out so we can see the color. I want it to look festive in the true Chilloween spirit."

"Right," Jackson said drily. "A holiday tradition for five minutes now."

"Don't make fun," Taylor pleaded. "I want this to be perfect!"

Jackson put one of the coolers up on the platform, then stood carefully on top of it. He teetered precariously as he fought to get the parachute stretched out.

"I thought Chillopalooza was supposed to be about kicking back," Jackson said, after wrestling with the parachute for a while.

"Kick later," Taylor said. "There's too much to do. Plus, it's *ween*. Chillo*ween*."

Jackson was sweating and his face looked a little pale.

"You okay?"

Jackson jumped down from the cooler he'd been standing on and sat for a moment. "Yeah," he said. "I gotta admit, I'm not much of a holiday guy. Honestly?" He looked up at Taylor. "No offense, but this seems kinda silly."

Taylor felt a flash of anger. But—uncharacteristically—she stifled it.

"Everybody here is good at something," she said. "Nathan is so eager and strong. Daley's perfect . . . sort of."

Jackson laughed.

"And Lex," she continued, "he's this little genius. Melissa's so sweet and keeps us together. Eric is, well, Eric's a rat. But he's good at it. And you're like . . . some kind of Yoda. Then there's me. I don't have a lot to offer."

"That's not true."

"It is! But there *is* something I'm good at. I know how to throw a party and have fun."

Jackson gave her brief smile, then stood up, walked a short distance from the shelter, and looked back. "Looks nice," he said.

"Thank you," Taylor said.

He gave her a sly smile. "Chillo . . . what is it again?"

"Chilloween."

Lex was looking for somebody to show off what he'd just accomplished. He found Melissa on the trail coming out of the woods. She was carrying the reflective piece of metal that Eric had been trying to make into a fire-starter earlier in the day.

"Hey, guess what?" Lex called enthusiastically.

She turned and put her finger to her lips, then pointed at the plane. He frowned, looking to see what she was pointing at.

Then he noticed Eric walking stealthily toward the airplane, carrying a small backpack. He looked from side to side, apparently making sure nobody was looking. Then he darted into the wreckage.

"*Now* what's he doing?" Lex said.

Melissa watched intently.

Eric soon burst out of the plane. He had something in his hand, but he was busy stuffing it in the backpack, so it was impossible to tell what it was.

"I really hope he's not going to ruin the holiday," Melissa said.

"So . . . I wanted to show you something," Lex said.

"Great," she said. "Catch me in a few minutes. I want to see what he's up to." Then she hurried over toward the airplane.

Melissa rushed across the sand and followed Eric into the woods. "Eric!" she called. "Hey! Eric!"

He froze, then turned around. He had a look on his face like, *busted!*

"What are you doing?" Melissa asked with

suspicion. She didn't like thinking badly of people. But Eric was getting on her last nerve. He never thought about anybody but himself.

"Nothing!" Eric said.

"What's in the pack?"

"Huh? Uh . . ." His eyebrows lowered. "Hey, you don't think I'm doing something wrong, do you?"

"I didn't say that," Melissa said.

"But you're thinking it!"

Melissa took a deep breath. "Okay. What *are* you doing?"

Eric rolled his eyes. "Unbelieveable!"

Then he turned and walked away in a big huff. Melissa watched him go. Definitely. He was definitely up to something. Then she heard footsteps behind her. She turned. It was Lex.

"Where's Eric?" Lex said.

Melissa pointed down the trail that led to Lex's garden.

"Oh, man," Lex said.

"What?" Melissa said.

Lex didn't answer, just headed down the trail. She followed. Soon they emerged into the clearing. Eric was crouched over near the garden, putting something into a bush.

"I don't believe it!" Lex said. Lex stormed out of the jungle toward Eric. Melissa continued to follow him.

"Are you stealing again?" Lex shouted.

Eric looked up with a start. "Huh?" Eric said.

"Again?" Melissa said. She turned to Eric. She had totally had it up to here with this guy. "What did you steal before?"

Eric jumped away from whatever it was that he had been stuffing under the bush, still holding his backpack. Eric glanced furiously at Lex. "You told her, Lex?" he said incredulously.

Lex looked embarrassed about something. Melissa frowned. What was going on here?

"Uh . . . no, I didn't," Lex said. "I just . . ."

Melissa put her hands on her hips. "What did you steal, Eric?"

Lex looked stricken. "I'm sorry, Eric. I didn't mean to tell, it just came out."

Eric's face hardened. "I thought you were a good guy, but you're just a little snitch."

"Stop talking to Lex like that," Melissa demanded, "and tell me what you did."

Eric clamped his mouth shut.

"It's nothing," Lex said. "Eric took some stuff— borrowed it, really—a couple of days ago. But he put it back. I promise, Eric, I didn't mean to tell."

"But you did, didn't you? Thanks, Lex. Glad to know I can trust you."

Melissa stared at him. "It was you, wasn't it?"

"Huh?" Eric said.

"Lex didn't just find those pills in his backpack. You took them, didn't you?"

Eric ground his teeth together, then whipped around and walked away. "Happy Chilloween, guys!" he yelled acidly. "Happy freakin' Chilloween."

Melissa stared after him, open-mouthed. She couldn't believe it. He'd had those pills all the time?

⊕

Daley was not the world's biggest fan of holidays. Her mom had been diagnosed with cancer when Daley was in sixth grade, then she had battled the disease for three years. Every holiday for those three years there had been this gloomy feeling, like, *This might be the last one.*

And finally it was. She remembered her mother at that final Thanksgiving. She'd worked so hard to look strong for Daley and her father. But everybody in the house knew how much it was costing her to pretend everything was normal. She'd made the turkey and the dressing and the mashed potatoes and on and on. Daley's mom had not been that great a cook, but that Thanksgiving she'd gone all out.

In fact, it was probably the best meal she'd ever cooked.

But it had taken all her strength to get it on the table. They'd said grace and her dad had ceremoniously poured this fancy wine. Then he poured sparkling grape juice in a wineglass for Daley. The decorations had been perfect, the food had been perfect. Everything was perfect.

Except that her mom was dying.

After all the preparations were complete, her mother had taken about two bites and said, "Okay, guys, I guess I better lie down."

And the last Christmas? Forget it. Pure misery.

Daley couldn't enjoy the food, couldn't enjoy the presents, couldn't enjoy anything. All she could do was feel guilty. *Why am I so healthy while Mom's sitting there looking like a wax dummy—* her cheeks sunken, her eyes surrounded by dark circles, her hair just growing back from the last round of chemo . . .

It was miserable.

Taylor had assigned Daley to prepare coconuts. So that's what Daley was doing. Breaking coconuts with a rock. Impaling the eyes with a stick. Hacking the husks off with the machete. Dumping out the coconut milk. It was hard, messy, tedious work.

"Careful," a voice said as she was bashing away at a coconut with the big rock. "You're gonna smash your hand."

Daley looked up. It was Nathan. He was cradling his right arm with his left.

Daley dropped the rock, wiped her brow. "I hate holidays," she said.

Nathan dropped down glumly next to her.

"What's wrong?" she said.

"I'm *so* close!" he said.

"To what?"

"Fire." Nathan massaged his elbow. "I keep getting smoke. But I just can't seem to get enough of a coal going. Just about the time that I get smoke, my arm gives out on me. You remember how I messed it up in football last year? Well, it's in the exact same place."

"You want me to try?"

"I guess." Nathan sighed loudly.

Suddenly Melissa burst out of the trees. "You will *not* believe this!" she said.

TWENTY-TWO

Melissa took the reflective metal sheet back to the plane and sat down with it. She'd been a little disappointed with everybody's reactions when she told them about Eric stealing the medicine.

Daley and Nathan had seemed all preoccupied. Taylor was so into her decorating that she didn't seem to care. And Jackson—Jackson was the one who could have died. And all he did was shrug and say, "Hey, all's well that ends well."

Chilloween. The whole thing was stupid. If she'd been able to cook . . . well, maybe it would have been a little cooler. But there was no fire. Cutting up little slivers of fruit? That didn't exactly qualify as cooking.

She sighed. She did have an idea, though.

When she baked cookies, she always used a

rolling pin to roll out the dough. She went into the wreckage and rooted around until she found a piece of steel tubing that was about the right size. It had been part of a chair that had gotten smashed up in the crash.

She took it outside, pressed the metal sheet against the flat skin of the airplane, then rolled the steel tube back and forth against the sheet.

Hey! she thought. *This actually works!*

Within a minute or two, the metal sheet was nice and smooth and reflective. Now all she had to do was turn it into a gently curved surface that would gather the sun and focus it onto one spot. She had seen this show on the Food Network once about how pots and pans were made. They took a sheet of steel and pressed it down into a form with this giant machine. If only she had the right form, she could just keep whacking the thing with a blunt stick until—

Suddenly an idea struck her. What about the nose cone of the plane? It seemed like it would be the right shape. Daley had taken it off and used it to wash clothes in.

She hurried over to the fire ring and found the nose cone lying on the sand. She set the metal sheet inside the nose cone and then began pushing and poking and banging with the walking stick that Lex had brought back after his trek into the woods.

After about twenty minutes of banging, it was

clear she'd made about as much p.
was going to. Then she took a woo
spoon that Jackson had carved and
around on the metal, trying to burnis
smooth it down as much as possible.

When she was done, she pulled the pie
metal out and held it up to the sun. Unfortunate.
was late in the afternoon and the sun was startin,
to get pretty far down on the horizon. She had a
hunch that even if everything worked right, she'd
still have to wait until tomorrow morning when
the sun was stronger to actually be able to start a
fire. Then she stuck her hand in front of the metal,
moving it back and forth to see if there was any
sort of focal point.

"Ow!" she shouted.

Her hand had gotten very hot.

Maybe I'm onto something! she thought.

She ran down to the shoreline and stuck her
hand in the water to cool it. Whew! That felt better.
The water felt so good that she waded in up to
her waist.

When she got back out, she realized that the
sun had gone down just far enough so that she
wasn't going to be able to use the reflector again
until morning. Unless . . .

There was a tiny scrap of sunlight coming
through a gap in the trees. She scooped up the
reflector and ran toward the bright spot on the
sand.

If only I had something that would burn ...

She patted her pants pockets. But they were all wet. What about her shirt? In the pocket of her flannel shirt, she found a tiny scrap of pink paper.

Well, she thought ... *it's not gonna work. But why not give it a try?*

Lex had been trying to tell everybody about his flint and steel all afternoon. But nobody seemed to be interested. Everybody was running around like chickens with their heads cut off, trying to get ready for this dumb, made-up holiday that nobody seemed to be interested in celebrating.

Oh, well, he thought. *Guess I'll just have to do this myself.*

Nathan was sitting next to the fire ring looking at his bow-and-drill. He kept getting smoke ... but then his arm would give out.

As he was staring at the bow, Taylor appeared. "What are you doing?" she said cheerfully. "You should be decorating or something!"

Nathan sighed, picked up the bow, and started sawing back and forth. "I'm getting so close," he said. He went faster and faster. A wisp of smoke appeared. Then he gasped and quit.

"See?" he said. "I'm about to blow out my elbow."

"That's because you're over-bowing," she said.

"I'm what?"

"Here, lemme see it," Taylor said.

"Takes a while to get the feel for it," Nathan said.

Taylor took the bow, the drill, and the two pieces that held the ends of the rotating stick, then looked around.

"What are you looking for?" Nathan said.

"A better place to set it up," Taylor said.

"It's fine on the ground," he said.

Taylor shook her head. "Nah. Not so much." Then she spotted something. "Oh, okay, here."

She sat down on a stump, then put everything together so the lower end of the drill was sitting in her lap. "See?" she said. "Like playing a cello. You want to have good posture, so you're not all hunched over."

Then she started moving the bow slowly back and forth.

"Too slow," Nathan said.

Taylor smiled, closed her eyes, and started running her hand back and forth. She looked just like she was playing a cello. After a minute, she started humming.

"Faster," Nathan said.

But Taylor ignored him, continuing to hum as she moved the bow back and forth, back and forth, back and forth. He had to admit, it looked completely effortless the way she did it. His approach had been like a sprint. After a short intense burst, he was always worn out. Thing is, he was sure that was what it took. At this rate she'd never produce any . . .

"Smoke!"

Nathan turned and saw Melissa standing on the edge of the clearing. He didn't know when she had stopped working on the reflector, but now she was holding a bunch of bright-colored flowers and pointing at Taylor's lap.

"She's getting smoke!" Melissa repeated.

Taylor swayed back and forth and suddenly there was quite a substantial cloud of smoke coming up from her lap.

"Great job, Taylor," Melissa said. "What do you want me to do with these flowers?"

"Flowers?" Taylor's eyes snapped open. "Omigod! I totally forgot about the flowers!"

Taylor hopped up and dropped the bow-and-drill set on the floor.

"Come with me, right this second," Taylor commanded Melissa. "I know exactly where those are gonna go."

Seconds later, they were all gone. Nathan ran over and picked up the fire-starting gear. It was only when he'd gotten it into his hands that he saw something. There, in the hollow of the lower drill receptacle was . . .

. . . a tiny, glowing ember.

He began to blow gently. "Come on, baby," he said softly. "Come on . . ."

As Lex was walking down the beach, he saw two pieces of wire lying in a bucket of water. One was red, the other white. They looked suspiciously like the leads off the back of the solar battery charger. That was strange. Why would anybody have cut them off?

He carried the wires down to the girls' tent, where he found the charger. Sure enough, the wires had been snipped off right at the ends. How dumb.

He reached into his pocket, took out the little multi-tool knife that his mother had given him before the trip, and pulled out the Phillips-head screwdriver. Then he unscrewed the back of the charger. Inside were two small terminals, one negative, one positive. It was the work of about two minutes to strip the ends of the two wires he'd found, place them under the terminals, and tighten them.

He smiled at his handiwork as he replaced the back of the charger. Good as new!

"You fixed it?"

He turned and found Daley looking at him.

"Sure, nothing to it."

Daley heaved a sigh of relief. "We thought it was broken for good."

Lex folded up his multitool and put it back in his pocket. "So, look, Daley," he said. "I've got a problem."

"Okay."

"Well, I found flint while I was gone."

"You *did*? Why didn't you tell us?"

"I tried to. As usual, you didn't listen. Anyway, I've managed to get sparks."

"Hey, that's great!"

"Yeah, but I can't get the sparks to ignite anything."

"Oh, there's a trick to it. You need piece of charred cloth. You put it under the sparks and it'll create this little ember. You blow on the ember, then stick some tinder on it."

"How do you know this?" Lex said.

"I read it in . . . uh . . ." Daley's face went red. She seemed suddenly to be embarrassed.

"What?" Lex said.

"I read it in a book about this girl that got kidnapped by Indians."

"Oh," Lex said. "Cool." Then his face fell. "I don't suppose we have any charred cloth around here, huh?"

"Well, as a matter of fact . . ." Daley said.

TWENTY-THREE

As the sun started to disappear behind the trees, Taylor gathered everyone at the fire pit. Taylor wore flowers in her hair and a brightly colored dress. Her hair was shining, and she wore makeup and her fingernails were painted. Nathan had almost forgotten how she normally looked.

Of course, the idea of normality almost seemed like a smack in the face, a reminder that nothing would ever be normal as long as they were stuck on this stupid rock.

"Happy Chilloween!" Taylor called. "As you all know, Chilloween officially starts when the sun goes below the horizon!"

Nobody responded to Taylor. The rest of the group just looked morosely at the horizon. The darkening sky seemed to only highlight their general mood. No one seemed excited except Taylor.

There was a large pyramid of wood in the middle of the fire ring. But it was not lit. A wind gusted off the ocean, making Nathan feel cold and clammy.

"This is so exciting, guys!" Taylor said. "I don't know about you, but I had a great day."

Again, nobody reacted.

"Let's see," Nathan said, "Lex got lost in the jungle, Jackson almost died . . ."

"We have no fire and no light," Eric said.

"No water," Nathan added.

"Oh, and by the way, we're stuck on a deserted island," Daley said.

Taylor held up her hands. "Come on, stick with me here! For our first surprise, Lex has rewired the sound system!" She turned and hit a button on the mp3 player. It began to play a lively song that had been popular back home.

"Good, huh?" Taylor said. "Festive!"

But then the sound grew quieter and the mp3 player started cutting out.

"Uh . . . I forgot to tell you, the batteries are about dead," Lex said.

Taylor smiled gamely. "Well, who cares! Look at the gorgeous meal that Melissa made for us." She pointed at the tray laid out next to the fire ring. On it lay a bunch of artfully arranged fruit.

"Yay," Eric said. "Fruit. How special."

Nathan was annoyed that Eric was making light of all Melissa's hard work on the fruit tray. But he had to admit, he agreed. This was not much of a meal.

"Now, before we eat . . . presents!" Taylor said. Despite the mood of the group, she forged on. "Who wants to go first?"

Melissa stood up shyly. "Well, it's not much. But I did sketches for everybody using charcoal from the fire. The . . . uh . . . dead fire."

She handed out small charcoal sketches of each of the members of the group. Nathan was amazed—as always—by how well she drew. She really had a gift for capturing something about the personality of everybody she sketched.

"Wow, Melissa," Daley said. "These are really good."

"I was kinda hoping for socks and underwear," Eric said.

"But there's more!" Taylor said. "Melissa isn't the only artist. Look! Jewelry!" She held up several small necklaces and bracelets. "Necklaces for the girls, bracelets for the guys. Aren't they awesome?"

Nathan examined the little bracelet Taylor gave him. It was made from a wire and tiny multicolored shells. "That is awesome, Taylor," he said. "Thanks."

"Who's next?" Taylor said.

Eric stood up. He took out his backpack and

opened it, revealing a large metal cone.

"What is it?" Lex said.

"You know, maybe you're not as smart as you think." He held up the cone and said, "If there's one thing we've got plenty of, it's sunshine. This is the thingamajig that protects the engine."

"Oh, yeah," Lex said. "I believe it's called a nacelle."

"Thank you, boy genius." Eric gave Lex a phony smile. "Anyway, this is the one of the doodads that goes around the engines. I figure if we hang this up, rainwater will collect in it and the sun will heat it. See these holes drilled in the bottom? You pull this handle and—"

"A shower!" Taylor shouted. "Eric, you are the best!" She grabbed him and hugged him.

Eric's eyes widened, then he grinned and hugged her back.

"Okay!" Taylor said, pulling away quickly. "Boundaries, Eric. Boundaries."

"Will it work?" Nathan said.

Lex leaped up to look at it. "Yeah, it'll work! Why didn't I think of this?"

"Because you were too busy spying on me," Eric said sourly. "What do you think I was carrying out there into the woods?"

"I'm sorry, Eric," Lex said.

"Me too," Melissa said.

"Yeah, right," Eric said.

"Who's next?" Taylor said. She was still smiling

broadly. But her smile was starting to look a little artificial. "Daley?"

Nathan looked expectantly at Daley. Daley looked around the circle. "Uh ... I guess I forgot. I didn't really think anybody else would . . ."

Nathan had somehow been expecting Daley to do something nice for him. They had been getting closer and closer to each other. And now she hadn't even remembered to do *anything*? Not even for him?

"Typical," Nathan said. "Always thinking about your own little problems."

Daley jumped up and ran off. She was clearly upset. Now Nathan felt like a jerk. But he was still a little mad, too.

"Just like the holidays at home," Eric said. "Somebody always runs off crying."

"Stop, Eric!" Melissa said. "We said we were sorry, so lighten up!"

"If anybody's gotta lighten up, it's you guys."

"Guys! Guys?" Taylor was looking a little desperate now. "We're trying to have fun here."

"Maybe this Chillout thing wasn't such a great idea, after all," Nathan said.

"Chilloween!" Taylor said. "Chillo*ween*."

There was a long silence.

"Has anybody got anything else?"

"Actually, yeah," Nathan said. He had one thing. Not that it would really turn things around. But it would help a little.

"Me too," Jackson said.

"Yeah," Lex said. "I've got something."

"I have something else," Melissa said. She looked at Eric. "Why don't you come with me . . ."

Everybody stood up to go. Nathan dusted the sand off his pants. Taylor was sitting gloomily at the edge of the cold, dark fire ring, her chin on her hands.

"Well," Nathan said. "You tried."

A tear ran down the side of her nose as he walked away.

TWENTY-FOUR

Taylor sat motionless for a long time. Eventually Jackson walked over, smiling tentatively.

"Well," he said. "At least we can have a little music. That's something, huh?"

Taylor shrugged.

He cleared his throat, then started humming. Taylor closed her eyes. She missed her cello.

She thought about being home. It was the weirdest thing. Not that she wanted to be stuck here, exactly. But in a strange kind of way, life was easier here than it was at home. She didn't have to be some fake version of herself here. At home she'd felt like she was putting on some kind of show all the time. Here? Well, it was just different.

Suddenly Jackson stopped humming.

"What?" she said.

But Jackson didn't start again.

She opened her eyes and saw something strange. It looked like . . .

Light.

Moving toward her across the beach was what looked like a torch. She turned to look at Jackson and saw . . . *more light*! Another torch was bobbing toward her from out of the jungle. And then another. And then another! Where was it coming from?

Suddenly everyone was standing around the circle staring at one another.

"What the . . ." Jackson said.

Nathan was holding a torch. He said, "I made fire today. But I couldn't have done it if Lex wasn't the world's worst Elvis impersonator."

Everyone laughed quizzically.

"Huh?" Lex said.

"Your microphone. It was the perfect kind of wood to make fire with." He turned to Taylor. "And you, Taylor. If you hadn't been a cello player? I'd have never figured out the technique. So anyway, after I got my fire started, I boiled some water." He set a jug down. "Drink up!"

"I made fire, too," Melissa said, holding up her torch. "With the last few rays of the sun. The reflector was Eric's idea. All I did was add a couple of things I knew about cooking to make the reflector work. Thanks, Eric."

Everyone looked at Eric. He was holding a large platter. Taylor's mouth was suddenly watering. "Is that what I think it is?" Taylor said.

"Grilled fish in coconut sauce!" Eric said, grinning. "Thanks, Melissa."

"I made fire with the flints I found when I got lost," Lex said. "But I couldn't have done it if Nathan hadn't loaned me his knife. And if Daley hadn't showed me a way of starting fires that she found . . ." He grinned. "I think she got it out of one of those dumb books she's always pretending not to read."

"What!" Daley said.

Everybody laughed again. Suddenly the mood was lightening.

"Thanks, Nathan," Lex said. "Thanks, Daley."

They smiled back at Lex.

"So anyway," Lex said. "I made everybody some candles. Daley, could you help me hand them out?"

Daley handed the first one to Nathan. "Sorry," she whispered.

He smiled back. "Hey, don't even think about it," he said softly.

"So I just have one question," Taylor said. "While I was decorating, there was no wood in the fire ring. But then when I came back, suddenly . . ." She gestured at the perfectly stacked wood in the middle of the ring. "Who did this?"

Everybody in the group shook their heads.

Everybody except Jackson.

Suddenly they were all looking at him. He grinned for a moment, then whistled nonchalantly.

"Why don't we all light the fire?" Jackson said. He took a small stick off the edge of the fire and lit the end of it from Melissa's torch.

Everyone else who wasn't holding a torch silently took a small stick and lit it from someone else's torch.

Taylor leaned toward the fire.

"Happy Chilloween!" she said.

"Happy Chilloween!" everyone else repeated.

And with that, they all put their torches or their sticks into the fire. In seconds the center of the fire had burst into flame. The fire quickly spread, and soon a cheerful blaze was crackling and snapping at the center of the fire ring.

"How did you know?" Melissa said to Jackson. "How did you know we'd all figured out different ways to start a fire?"

He shrugged. "What can I say? I had confidence in you."

Everyone looked around at one another.

"Wow," Melissa said.

"Remember what I said yesterday? If everybody throws away the rule book and does stuff they really enjoy? I knew we'd figure out a way to do it."

Heads nodded around the fire.

"How did you get to be so wise?" Taylor said. "I mean, seriously?"

Jackson cleared his throat. "Plus, uh . . ." He reached into his pocket, pulled something out, and flicked it. A tiny flame appeared in his hand. "I had three lighters."

The entire group groaned.

"Oh, man! You're such a jerk!" Nathan hurled a piece of fruit at Jackson, who dodged it, grinning. Everyone dissolved into laughter.

Taylor felt a glow of contentment. *I did this!* she thought. *I did this.* She couldn't believe it. Suddenly everyone was smiling and laughing, their faces lit up—not just with the fire—but with happiness.

"Let's eat!" Melissa said as she circled the ring, pouring everyone a coconut shell full of water.

"Hold on a second," Jackson said. "Lex, Nathan told me about your bird. It sounds like the bird must have run into Captain Russell and the others. So . . . here's a toast—not just to us, but to Captain Russell and Jory and Ian and Abby." Jackson hoisted his glass into the air. "Happy Chilloween!"

The whole group reached for the cups of water and held them in the air.

"Happy Chilloween!"

Change is coming to the island—change that could tear apart the castaways. Will they be able to hold onto all that they've built, or is it too late to even try? Turn the page for a sneak peek at *Flight 29 Down #7: Survival* . . .

ONE

DAY NINE ON THE ISLAND

Nathan walked out of the boys' tent and stretched. It was another beautiful day on the island. In front of him lay the long white beach where he and his friends had crash-landed just a little over a week earlier.

One day he kept thinking he'd wake up lying in his own bed, and this would all turn out to be a dream.

He sighed. Another day stuck on this island "paradise."

As he started walking over toward the other tent where the water was stored, he noticed a girl's necklace lying on a chair they'd pulled out of the wreck of flight 29 DWN. It was a simple gold chain with one of those swirly yin-yang symbols on it. Didn't Abby Fujimoto wear a necklace like that?

Next to the necklace was a book with the word JOURNAL printed on the front in neat black letters. It seemed to have been intentionally left where everybody would see it.

As he picked up the necklace to examine it more closely, Nathan heard someone else approaching. He looked up and saw Daley coming toward him, yawning and raking her fingers through her wavy red hair.

"Where's Abby?" Nathan said.

"She's sleeping," Daley said.

"No, she's not," Melissa said, emerging from the girls' tent.

Nathan picked up the journal and noticed a piece of paper tucked between the pages. It read, "Read this."

"Hey, look," he said. "She left us a note."

Taylor popped out of the tent. Unlike everybody else—who looked like they had just woken up—Taylor's hair somehow managed to look perfect. "Hey!" she said. "Where's my backpack? My eyeliner is in there."

Nathan opened the journal and started reading aloud. It was Abby's graceful handwriting. "'Please forgive me,'" he read. "'This is something I have to do. Jackson, I believe you; it's about right here, right now. And right now I've got to find the others.'"

Nathan was stunned. Abby had left the camp on the first day with the pilot, Captain Russell, and two other kids from the Hartwell School, Ian and Jory. She had gotten separated from them, then fought her way back to camp. Why would she leave again? After all that she'd gone through out there in the woods, you'd think she would have wanted to stay with the group.

"She took my backpack?" Taylor said. "I can't believe she took my eyeliner. This is a *disaster*!"

Nathan kept reading. "'Please don't follow me. I'll be fine. I know you'll understand because you'd do the same if one of you were lost. I'm going to find Captain Russell and the others, and I'm going to bring them back. Try not to worry. Make more happy memories. Love, Abby.'"

Nathan looked up at his friends. "We have to go after her!"

Jackson shook his head. "No, we don't."

Sometimes Nathan just didn't get Jackson. It was obvious that Abby was going to be in a lot more danger if she was out there by herself in the jungle than if she were here with everybody else. Ian and Jory were with Captain Russell. He was a grown-up. He'd take care of them. Why did she want to risk her neck for no reason?

"What if she gets lost again?" Nathan said to Jackson.

Jackson spread his hands. "What are we gonna do, Nathan? Drag her back? Tie her to a tree? If she wants to go, she'll just go again."

Melissa frowned thoughtfully. "Maybe we could help her find the others!" she said.

"Yeah," Eric said sarcastically. "Then maybe we could get ourselves lost, too."

Taylor looked around the group. "So what do we do?"

The youngest member of the group, Daley's little brother, Lex, piped up. "She knows the island," he said matter-of-factly. "She'll come back. Eventually."

"Hopefully they'll all come back," Daley said.

Nathan shook his head. He didn't like it. All this lone hero stuff got people in trouble. It had been nine days since Captain Russell and the others had left. Only Abby had come back. The island wasn't *that* big. He was afraid something bad had happened to them. No, sticking together and hunkering down until they got rescued—that was their only hope.

But Abby was gone now. The truth was, there wasn't much they could do for her now.

Jackson looked off toward the trees. "Good luck, Abby," he said softly.

TWO WEEKS LATER: THE PRESENT

Eric

Dude, I am *sick* of this! It's been, like, three weeks now.

When do we start giving up hope of rescue? A week? A month? Hey, come on, we're fooling ourselves if we think every boat in the Pacific Ocean is looking for us anymore. I bet it was probably a big deal at first. Kids disappear into the ocean, blah blah blah—I'm sure all the news channels were talking about nothing else ... for about ten minutes.

But then something else happened. Some famous actor got arrested for acting weird at the mall or something—and, boom, we're yesterday's news.

"Oh, yeah, those kids on the plane? Did anybody ever find them? I can't remember."

Nobody cares anymore. Except maybe our parents. And what can they do? Even Taylor's dad, who's, like, one of the richest guys in California. What's he gonna do—hire every airplane in the world to search the entire Pacific Ocean? Don't think so.

I think we're kidding ourselves with this whole sit-around-and-wait routine. It's time to stop dreaming and start thinking up a way to get out of here.

After he switched off the video camera, Eric felt a little deflated. It was all well and good to say he wanted to do something about getting rescued. But ... like what?

It wasn't like he was an airplane mechanic.

And they didn't exactly have a boat handy.

He set the camera down by the shelter they'd built a few days back and walked disconsolately along the shoreline. Off in the distance, everybody was all busy and cheerful looking. Daley and Nathan were doing their busy-bee routine, working on some kind of little helpful project. Melissa was cooking. Lex was carrying a handful of fruit back out of the forest. He could hear the sound of Jackson's machete hacking away back in the trees. Jackson had been sick as a dog with this stomach bug called giardia only a couple of days ago, but he still was trying to pitch in. Even Taylor was down at the far end of the beach fishing.

He kept walking glumly, kicking the sand as he went.

Then he spotted something washing up on the shore. A scrap of wood. It wasn't just some tree that had fallen in the ocean. It was lumber, a board. Man-made.

He grabbed it and picked it up. There was some writing on it.

Whoa! he thought as he read the script inked onto the side of the wood. An idea started forming in his mind.

Maybe this was the answer to their problems!

He began to run back toward the camp. "Hey!" he called. "Hey! Guys!"

"How many did you get?" Daley said as Taylor walked back into camp. Taylor was carrying a stick with some silvery fish skewered on it.

Taylor held up the stick. "Only two. It seems like we've caught most of the good ones in that shallow area down there. We may need to start fishing farther down the beach."

Daley sighed loudly. It was a recurring theme. They seemed to have gathered most of the food within a reasonable distance of their camp. They were having to travel farther and farther distances every day to find anything edible.

"Hey!" a voice called. "Check this out!"

Eric burst into the camp waving . . . well, it looked like a piece of wood.

"Wow!" Taylor said. "A piece of slimy, gross-looking old board. How fascinating."

Eric didn't seem to be bothered by Taylor. "Look." He tapped his finger on the wood. Daley could see that something was printed on the board. "Right here!"

Nathan leaned toward it and squinted at the board. "'Marianas Shipping. Agana Harbor. Guh.'" He looked up. "Guh? What's guh?"

"Not *guh*." Eric kept waving the board excitedly. "G-U. See where the board's broken? If it wasn't broken, it would say G-U-A-M. Guam!"

Taylor looked around blankly. "Clueless," she said.

Lex joined them from the path and said, "It probably floated here on the current."

"Exactly! Extra bonus for Boy Brainiac." Eric clapped Lex on the shoulder. "I've always said we should listen to this kid more often."

"No, you haven't," Taylor said. "Usually you say he's an annoying—"

Eric waved his hands, cutting her off. "Never mind that. Point is, if this thing made it all the way from Guam, then there's a serious current going past the island."

Daley was not following him. Obviously there were currents in the ocean. That was hardly big news. "So what?" she said.

"Hello!" Eric stared at her like she was a moron. "Currents don't stop. They keep on . . . currenting. If it can carry a piece of wood this far, it might carry something bigger."

Nathan scratched his head. "Like . . . a really big piece of waterlogged junk?"

"Come on! Like . . . a *raft*. With us on it."

Daley scoffed. Eric was always looking for a magic bullet. Instead of doing sensible, normal hard work. Like cooking. Or gathering food. Or tending the fire, or—

"You're kidding, right?" Nathan said, anticipating Daley's next words.

"Hmm . . ." said Melissa. "Gee, that sounds kind of ambitious."

"A raft?" Taylor said. "Like, in the water?"

"Not gonna happen, Eric," Daley added.

"Why not?" Eric said.

There was a moment of silence. Finally Nathan said, "Uh, there's a whole bunch of answers to that. Starting with certain death, right up there on the tippy-top of the list."

Eric's face was starting to get red. "We gotta face reality, people. It's been three weeks."

"And one day," Lex added.

"Yeah, okay, three weeks and one day," Eric pursued. "Whatever. What I'm saying is, if they were looking for us anywhere near here, we'd all be home sitting at the pool and sipping ice cold sodas. Best case scenario, they're looking in the wrong place. Worst case? Hey, our parents have all had memorial services for us and they're getting on with their lives. Face it, at some point, they're just gonna stop looking."

"Don't even think that!" Daley said. She was sick of Eric always undermining everybody's morale.

Eric's usually cocky expression faded. His voice grew quieter. "Guys, I want to keep hoping as much as anybody. Believe me, I do! But when do we start taking control of our lives?"

There was a brief silence.

"So you're really being serious?" Melissa said finally. "You really want to build a raft and float off into . . . whatever's out there?"

Eric cleared his throat. "Well, no. Not yet, anyway. I think we should build a small raft—for two people maybe. Just to see if we can do it. That way we can test the current."

"Test for what?" Daley said skeptically. Eric was always coming up with plans—but they were never practical.

"For direction," Lex said.

"Exactly!" Eric put up his hand as though to high-five Lex.

Lex didn't seem to see Eric's hand, though. Daley could tell that his mind was already working on the problem. Once that happened, Lex tended to lose awareness of his surroundings. "We flew west from Guam toward Palau," Lex said. "If that chunk of wood floated here on a western current, it might keep on going to Asia."

He picked up a stick and immediately started drawing something on the sand. A map, Daley assumed.

"And if it's an eastern current?" she said.

Nathan looked down at the map Lex was drawing. "If it goes east . . ." He pointed at the map. "If it goes east, it'll just dump smack into the middle of the Pacific."

Everyone looked glum. Which was okay with Daley. She didn't think this was such a hot idea, anyway.

"I'm only saying we do a test," Eric said. "Who knows? If we're stuck here for another couple of months, we might start getting desperate. At least we'd have a backup plan."

"I don't think we'd ever get that desperate," Daley said.

Eric looked her in the eye. "Fine. That's your opinion. Let's put it to a vote. Who's in favor of building a raft to test the currents?"

Eric raised his arm sharply in the air.

Daley looked around, expecting to see a solid show of disapproval. To her shock, Jackson, Lex, and Taylor slowly lifted their hands. She couldn't believe it! Every minute they invested in some nutty scheme like this was a minute that couldn't be spent fishing or gathering fruit or cleaning clothes or boiling safe drinking water.

"Seriously?" she said. "With all the important stuff we have to do around here? That's what you guys really want?"

Jackson shrugged.

Eric smiled smugly. "Four to three, baby. Four to three."

Daley looked at him sourly. "Fair enough," she said. "Four to three. We build a raft." She paused and looked around the group. "I just hope we're not making a huge mistake."

Daley

Democracy. That's what we agreed to.

But it makes me wonder how smart a democracy can be when the majority votes to do something so totally idiotic!

Okay, let's go with the idea. Let's say the current's going in the right direction. What then? We don't know a thing about how to make a boat that would hold up in a big storm. We've had three major storms since we've been here. We'd be pretty much guaranteed of getting hit with a big storm before we got to wherever we were going. The waves here are humongous. They'd tear a *real* boat apart. Much less a bunch of moldy old stuff held together with string and bubble gum.

And do we have any clue as to where we'd be going? Zero. We know squat about navigation. We have no motor. We don't even have sails. And even if we did, how do you even steer a raft?

And what about food? We have no way of storing food. Even if we could find enough extra food that we could spend weeks drying fruit and smoking fish . . . what then? We might be floating around out there for months. And then there's drinking water. No way in the world do we have enough room to store drinking water for a month or two.

It's crazy. It's just plain nuts!

TWO WEEKS EARLIER

This isn't so bad, Abby Fujimoto thought as she hiked through the forest. It was early in the day and the oppressive tropical heat hadn't set in yet. Multicolored birds flitted through the air overhead, their raucous calls echoing happily through the trees.

Everywhere she looked, the world seemed new and exciting. Abby's family did a lot of camping and hiking, and she had been raised to believe that people should live in harmony with the natural world. What was there to worry about here? She'd been separated from Captain Russell and the others in a freak accident. It wouldn't happen again.

This time it would be . . . well, maybe "fun" wasn't the right word. But it would be an interesting opportunity for personal growth. Right?

And not just that—she'd find the others and bring them back. Soon the whole group would be together. Maybe Captain Russell had figured out a way to get them off the island. Maybe all that was left to do was to reunite the two groups, and everything would be squared away again.

She hiked slowly up the next hill. The island was volcanic, so there were a lot of very steep hills. And this was the steepest one yet. *There's no rush,* she told herself. *It's all about the journey.* She pulled herself from tree to tree, vine to vine, rock to rock. When she needed a rest, she stopped briefly and took deep, cleansing breaths.

This was so much better, she thought, than sitting around cooped up in the camp with all the petty little jealousies and conflicts, waiting and waiting and waiting. Here, she felt like she was moving forward, making progress.

Finally she topped the rise, finding herself with a breathtaking view of the island. She surveyed the scene. From here she could see the mountain at the far end of the island. It was a little farther away than she'd thought. Higher, too. The flat, volcanic rim at the top was shrouded in clouds. A small waterfall cascaded over the side, the water turning to mist as it fell toward the emerald green jungle below.

How many kids get to see something like this? she thought. *I must be the luckiest girl in the world.* Eventually they'd all get off the island, and she'd look back at this moment as one of the best things that ever happened in her life.

On the far side of the mountain she could see a crescent-shaped lagoon. A perfect place for Captain Russell and the others to camp and prepare their plans for getting off the island. She wasn't absolutely sure that's where they were. But she had a pretty good idea they'd be there.

The mountain was a little worrisome. She was going to have to swing wider to get around the steep volcanic sides of the peak. She had thought it would only take a day or so to get to the lagoon. But now that she looked at it from here, she revised her plans. Maybe more like two days. Three, tops. But that was okay. She'd packed plenty of water.

Speaking of which . . .

Realizing the hiking had made her a little thirsty, Abby reached into her pack to pull out her water. She'd packed a couple of bottles, plus a larger gallon-size container. She grabbed one of the bottles, screwed the top off, and took a long swig.

Perfect.

She put the bottle back. As she reached inside, though, her hand came away wet. She frowned. That was odd.

She felt the bottom of the pack. It was soaked. Where was the water coming from? With a slight pang of nervousness, she tugged on the gallon jug. It offered strangely little resistance. It should have been a lot heavier!

Abby yanked the plastic jug out of the backpack and found to her horror that it had a tiny little cut in the bottom, so small that it only dripped at a very slow rate. It must have been leaking since the minute she'd left. And now there was barely more than a couple of mouthfuls sloshing around in the bottom.

She stared. For a moment she had the urge to panic.

Okay. Okay. Easy, Abby. No prob. Deep breaths. Think.

After a few deep breaths she felt better. All those yoga classes she'd gone to with her mother were paying off. No point stressing out, right? She still had two quarts of water. There were streams on the island. It rained all the time here. The lagoon was only a couple of days away. What was she worried about? There was water everywhere.

Still . . . the thought crossed her mind that she could go back to camp and get more. It would be a lot easier to do that than to have to fool around with finding water.

But then she thought, *No, they wouldn't understand. They'd make a big scene.* She hated that kind of drama. She was all about harmony.

She carefully repacked the two quart bottles of water and began descending the hill. Nothing to worry about. Nature would provide.

Abby smiled. *I'll be fine,* she thought. *Of course I will!*